They Call Me Zombie

John Mercer

Cover Design by Abigail Grimshaw

ISBN:1490970940
ISBN-13: 978-1490970943

For my Mom and Dad, who no doubt spent countless hours wondering what in the world they had done.

To My Friends at Fairmount Library –

THEY CALL ME
ZOMBIE

Hope You Have A

Scary Good Read!

John Mercer

ACKNOWLEDGMENTS

There are so many people who played such an important part in this book becoming a reality. Great Appreciation and Heartfelt Thanks go out to Kate, Sami, Lindsay, Justin, and Todd. Very Special Thanks to my friends Alex, Colleen, and Honey. Thank you Jim for all of your valuable insight and advice. And finally, thank you Donna, who was there every step of the way!

Prologue

Syracuse, New York

August 17th, 1999

The sound of boots on cement echoed down the long dimly-lit corridor of the Salt City Correctional Facility. The four men, dressed in standard guard uniforms, moved as one. They marched past the nine empty cells, moving toward the last remaining prisoner on death row.   In unison, the guards stopped in front of the cell. The lead guard, the oldest one with gray hair, stepped forward, removed a piece of paper from his pocket and began to read, while the other three fanned out across the cell bars.

"Travis Cleveland Riley, you have been convicted and found guilty by the state of New York for setting fire to the Mason Storage House. The fire in question led directly to deaths of two individuals inside the storage house. Your act of cowardice and your refusal to cooperate with authorities in this matter has led to your conviction. As such, the state of New York has hereby sentenced that you be electrocuted until dead."

From the darkened corner of his cell, Travis Cleveland Riley rose up and stepped to the center of his shadowy cage. His thin frame stood motionless in the half-light of the cell. He was not a large man or bulky with muscles, yet he was the one prisoner that both guards and inmates feared the most. The guard on the right, still safe behind the bars, started to tremble in a barely visible, yet uncontrollable shiver.

Travis stepped closer to the bars, his hard etched face

and black eyes becoming illuminated. There was a

dark and evil presence that emanated from him. It

was hard to explain, but anyone who met Travis

Cleveland Riley could feel it just as plain as a cold

November wind.

The lead guard who spoke stepped back from the

cell door and spoke again, "Unlock it, Jimmy."

"Yes Boss," The young guard nervously fumbled

with the keys. He stepped forward as his shaky hand

tried to insert the key into the lock. He missed twice,

then finally inserted the key, and the lock clicked.

Jimmy pulled the key out and stepped back quickly as

the cell door creaked slowly open. Travis Cleveland

Riley, already in handcuffs and leg cuffs, moved in measured steps toward the opening cell door. Travis paused and tilted his head, causing his neck to make a loud crack. He turned and, surrounded by the guards, shuffled down the corridor at a methodical pace.

At the end of the hallway the group turned right and exited through a locked door, out into the bright August afternoon. The coolness of the cement building was instantly gone, replaced by sweltering summer humidity. They proceeded across a small yard spotted with patches of burnt grass among the brown, dry earth. Keys jangled again, as the door to the brick building that was their destination was unlocked. Travis was escorted into a small room where the last working electric chair in New York State was bolted to the wooden floor.

Travis sat in the chair and as the guards strapped him in, they could feel his skin, cool and clammy. The lead guard checked all of the straps, redid the wrist strap that Jimmy had tied, and stepped in front of the seated prisoner.

"Travis Cleveland Riley, do you have any last words?" he asked.

Travis shifted slightly in the chair, causing all of the guards to step back. Despite the fact he was strapped to a chair that was bolted into the floor and hooked to electrodes with thousands of volts ready to rush through them, none of the men guarding him would feel safe until this was done. Travis turned his head to gaze at the clock on the wall and began to mumble.

"Twelve fifty nine and thirty seconds....thirty one seconds...thirty two seconds...."

The lead guard cleared his throat, "No last words."   He stepped off to the left, behind a heavy black curtain and stood before the control box.   Lifting the dark metal lever, he heard the generator begin to hum. He looked back, checking to make sure the other guards were safely away from the chair. Stepping once again behind the curtain, his gaze was fixed at the clock on the wall.   At exactly 1 pm he pulled the dark lever down and Travis Cleveland Riley fried.

Chapter 1

12 Years Later

There she was. Melissa Burns. She was thirteen, a year older than me. She was stepping into the pool and even though it was community swim and the pool was full of screaming kids, it was as if time froze while she gently waded into the water. The sun sent sparkles through the air and they all seemed to land on her lean, tan body which was already showing signs of curves, if you know what I mean. She was with her friends, Brenda and Jennica, but they were pretty much invisible next to Melissa. Her fingers brushed gently across the water as she laughed at whatever stupid thing Brenda had said. She flipped her head and her long blond hair flowed in slow motion back across her shoulders. She gazed around the edge of the pool and as her blue eyes drifted across the deck full of moms and kids, her eyes came to rest on mine and I'm sure I saw her smile. At me!

"Hey Mikey, take a picture, it'll last longer," laughed my best friend, Rosie, breaking my trance. Rosie was short for Carlos Rosario. Everyone calls him Rosie. And nobody, not even his mom calls him Carlos. He moved here in the third grade from Florida and we've been best friends ever since.

"Dude, she's way too hot for you," added my second best friend, Tom Porter. Tom and I have gone to the same school since kindergarten, but we really didn't start to hang out until the fifth grade. I guess the reason why is because I was always kind of a geek and Tom was always into sports. I would rather read a book or play a video game and Tom would rather kick a ball. It pretty much stayed that way until Tom broke his leg playing soccer. After that, Tom's mom decided that he was done with contact sports, and we started to hang out more often.

"She's amazing," I sighed. I watched as Melissa and the girls slowly drifted toward the deep end of the pool. This was pretty much how I've spent my summer vacation. Rosie and Tom and I would meet in the morning and head right for the pool to get the spot in back corner behind the deep end. We could see everything from there. And each day I would wait to see if the amazing Melissa Burns would be coming to the pool.

Tom looked down and started to pick at a scab on his knee. "If she's so amazing, why does she hang out with a loser like Brenda? Seriously, Brenda is so stuck up and she's not even that good-looking. It's like because she hangs out with Melissa she thinks she's hot, too. She's going to be in for a big surprise someday."

"What are you talking about?" Rosie asked.

"You ever hear of genetics? It means that when we get older, we all end up looking like our parents. You ever see Brenda's mom? She's so ugly, I get an allergic reaction just thinking about her." Tom's eyes popped open wide, his tongue rolled out of his mouth and he pretended to go into convulsions, his arms flapping wildly.

"I wouldn't say that too loud if I were you, Tom. If her brother hears you, he'll kill you," Rosie warned. "Seriously, I heard he killed a kid." Whenever he used the word "seriously," you knew Rosie was joking. But in this case, it might've been true. Brenda's brother, Craig, was the meanest kid in the school. Everyone thinks bullies are these giant, stupid doofballs. That couldn't be further from the truth about Craig, except the giant part. He was a bigger than average-sized eighth grader. He's so big, his muscles have muscles. He must have gotten all of the good genes in that family because he also looked like a model for one of those fancy men's magazines. All of the girls drool over him. He is also smart, so all of the teachers drool all over him, too. He should be covered in drool, but he isn't. Everybody loves him, which makes him even more dangerous, like a super-evil villain. He once beat up a kid and then convinced the teacher that the kid did it to himself. The kid got suspended for two days and had to go to counseling. Give me a giant doofus any day over a kid like Craig.

Tom finished with his scab, examined it, then tossed it over his shoulder and wiped the blood from his knee. "Hey, I got an idea. Why don't we cannonball the girls?"

"Ahhh, yeah!" Rosie agreed, sitting up and pulling his swim trunks up again. He got up to his knees, his tan belly still hanging over the edge of his shorts. Rosie has always been, well, let's say chunky. I only say that because that's what he says.

Now in my head I was thinking cannonballing the

girls, maybe wasn't such a good idea. What if Melissa gets mad or what if we get kicked out of the pool?

Rosie had a habit of reading my mind. "Listen, you want to get Melissa to notice you, right? And what's the worst they can do? There's only a week left of summer vacation. I say let's go bomb the girls!"

It was hard to argue with Rosie's logic. Now, I know what you must be thinking. What about the annoying Brenda and her psychotic bully brother? Weren't we afraid of what might happen if she got mad? That's a good question and one we should have thought about. I can't speak for the other guys, but the thought of getting close to Melissa outweighed any common sense I might have had at that moment.

We devised a quick plan. Tom would go at

them from the right, I would jump from the middle, and Rosie would land the mother of all cannonballs by jumping off the diving board. It was going to be epic.

Tom and Rosie both got up and began to move into position. After about five steps, Tom yelled something I couldn't hear and turned in a full sprint for the water. I sprang to my feet and began my run toward the girls. From the corner of my eye I watched as Rosie ran around the edge of the deck, his belly jiggling, heading for the diving board. I sprang from the cement and tucked my knees to my chest. Melissa Burns turned toward me, her mouth opened in shock, water splashing on her face from the impact of Tom's cannonball.

I hit the water with a mighty crash. Bubbles and

currents flowed all around me as I sank toward the bottom of the pool. As my feet finally touched bottom, I could hear muffled screams from Melissa and her friends. I pushed up from the bottom. As I ascended I wondered why I had not heard Rosie's explosion into the pool. I was starting to wonder if he had chickened out or got yelled at by the lifeguard. I was two strokes from the surface when Rosie broke the water. At almost the same instant, I felt the full weight of Rosie, 155 pounds of him, landing on my head. Air bubbles flew from my mouth and nose, my head snapped backward and I heard something crack in my neck. My arms and legs tingled like an electric shock went through them, then they went numb. I felt myself fall off to the side and I began to sink back down to the bottom of the pool. Ribbons of red, blood from my nose, lofted gently in the water. I remember

watching it rise, swirling like red smoke from a

cigarette as I drifted downward...downward, away

from the surface and away from the light.

Chapter 2

Beep. Beep. Beep.

Even before I opened my eyes I could hear the beeps from the machines that were hooked up to me. I realized I must be in a hospital, but I kept my eyes closed for a moment longer, checking to see what I felt. My throat was sore and dry.   My head and my neck didn't hurt but they felt stiff and heavy. Gradually, I opened my eyes.   The ceiling was a dull white. It definitely needed a paint job. I tried to turn my head, but it wouldn't move. Moving only my eyes, I looked off to my right and there was my mom, sitting asleep in a chair, a yellow blanket half covering her.

"Mom," my voice came out as a hoarse whisper. My throat burned and now I realized how sore it really was, like someone had taken a piece of sandpaper to it. I tried again. "Mom?"

Her eyes flickered open as she came awake. In a swift, flowing motion she rose from her chair, blanket falling to the floor and moved to the bed. She gently brushed her hand across my face and moved the hair off my forehead. She smiled sweetly at me, you know, one of those mom smiles.

"Hey Baby," she sighed. "How are you?"

Before I could answer she moved her hand into mine. "Can you squeeze my hand Mikey?" She asked, almost desperately. I squeezed her hand and her eyes began to well up with tears.

"Oh, thank God," she whispered.

Her breath smelled of coffee and her eyes looked tired.   She must have rushed to get here because I could tell that she wasn't wearing any make-up. I know women like make-up and all, but she always seemed to look better without it. It was a weird thing about my mom.

"Can I have a drink?" I managed to ask through the burning in my throat.

She lifted a cup of ginger ale and put the straw to my mouth. "Here you go. Just take small sips, okay?"

The bubbly ginger ale ran down the back of my throat, so cold and soothing, like a ginger ale waterfall. I wanted it to stay there and not keep going down to my stomach.   I tried to sip more but a sudden exhaustion swept over me like a wave. The straw slipped from my mouth.

"Mikey?" I heard my mom say. My eyes were closing again but I could tell she was now standing over me. I felt myself falling again like in the pool. I could hear my mom's frantic cries. "Mikey? Mikey! I need a doctor in here. HELP!"

Chapter 3

The sun was hanging in the sky like a giant orange balloon. As I looked around, I found myself standing out behind my Uncle Bob's barn.   It looked like one of those barns you'd see in a calendar from the bank. It had worn red paint and white trim, and it sat in a lush green field that led to a tree line in the distance. Uncle Bob wasn't a farmer. He was just a guy who had a huge barn in his enormous yard. Inside the barn were a couple of old cars, tons of tools and hundreds of boxes full of junk and treasure. I loved being here! It was one of my favorite places to go because I could go out and explore or play and no one ever bothered me. I could spend hours by myself, just being a kid. I started to laugh. I couldn't remember being so happy. I think the last time I was here was three years ago. Wait. Wasn't that for Uncle Bob's

funeral? Isn't Uncle Bob dead?

The sun was bright and I was warm, but

something still seemed off. I was wondering what I

was doing here when I heard a familiar bark. I turned

to look over my shoulder and racing around the corner

of the barn was my dog, Luther. He was a big black

lab. I couldn't believe it. I ran toward him, laughing,

and he ran right into me, knocking me to the ground.

One thing about Luther, he was a world champion

slobberer, and he was proving it right now. His rough

tongue was licking my face, making me laugh even

harder. I pushed him off and got to my feet, wiping

the drool away. There was a yellow tennis ball, already

covered in his slime sitting at my feet. I picked it up

and threw it into the field and Luther took off like a

28

shot. He retrieved the ball and returned to me, his tail wagging. I pulled it out from his slobbering mouth and threw it again. As I watched him chase after the ball, it suddenly occurred to me that I hadn't played catch with Luther in, well, forever. When was the last time we played catch? Wait Luther's been dead for three years? What was going on here?

"Mikey?"

"Mikey?" I heard the man's voice a second time, coming from behind me. My heart froze and from the inside out, I felt my whole body get goose bumps. I turned back toward the barn again. I could see the silhouette of a man outlined against the brilliant sunlight. I strained my eyes to see his face. I stepped closer.

"Dad?" I asked in a soft voice that begged for him to say yes. I stepped closer again but the light seemed brighter now. Then, without warning, the light exploded outward, all around and through me in blinding rays.

"Dad?" I yelled one last time as a giant ball of light flew forward, hitting me in the chest, knocking me backward through the air, sending me flying away from the barn.

Chapter 4

In an instant, I felt my body slamming back into the hospital bed, nearly knocking the wind out of me. Every part of my body tingled and I felt a strange sense of emptiness. I was happy where I had been, so why was I back here?

"Michael? Michael?"

I could hear a man's voice, so I opened my eyes. I was staring up at a doctor. He had the most nose hair I had ever seen in any human being. Not that I look at nose hair all the time, but this was growing out of his nose like a wild bush. I mean giant strands that curled and twisted everywhere and it was just inches above my face. If I could have moved, I would have bolted for the door.

31

"We've got him back," the doctor with the stringy nose hair shouted as he stood up, moving the nose hairs away from my view. He immediately barked out instructions to the nurses that were in the room. Most of it I didn't understand. He leaned back down, nose hairs getting closer, and shined a little flashlight into both of my eyes, which fortunately, temporarily blinded me from viewing them again. Then he pulled back and asked me how I was feeling.

"Kind of tired," I said. Realizing my throat was still scratchy as a cactus, I added, "I'm kind of thirsty too."

Dr. Nose Hair gave some more directions to the nurses and folded his arms. Looking at me he said, "You gave us quite a scare there Chief."

My mom pushed past a nurse, moving quickly to my bedside, tears in her eyes.

"Baby, are you okay?"

"Mom, I feel good. My throat is still sore and I'm really thirsty, but Mom, I'm better," I replied, trying to make her feel better too. Nobody wants to see their mom cry. But saying that only made her tears come down more. Women are pretty hard to figure out.

A nurse brought me some ginger ale and I sipped that golden liquid down. Then I remembered my dream. "Mom, I had the most amazing dream. It seemed so real. I was at Uncle Bob's house, out back by the barn. And Luther was there and we played catch and…"

I hesitated to tell her the next part, trying to decide if it

33

would make her cry even more or not. "I think I saw Dad there, too."

Mom stood up, wiped her eyes and stuck out her chin. I can tell when she does this she's got something to say that she doesn't really want to say. She calls this 'gathering her resolve.' I call it waiting for the bad news.

"Mikey, you weren't dreaming. You were dead."

That sounded so strange to me. "But I'm not dead now," I replied half as a statement and half as a question.

"No Mikey, you're safe now." She said, holding my hand in hers.

"I'm really tired. I'm going to sleep for a few minutes, Mom," I said as I squeezed her hand. I closed my eyes and drifted off.

Chapter 5

My eyes opened the next morning to see a blond-haired, blue-eyed princess smiling at me. On the wall to the left of her, a red-haired mermaid sat perched up on a rock and she was smiling too. A sickening feeling swept over me. They had placed me in the 'Princess Room' of the hospital. I could only pray that Tom and Rosie did not stop by to visit. I scanned the room to see three other cartoon princesses all smiling at me. Mocking me might be more like it.

As I was contemplating the endless teasing I would have to endure if my friends stopped by, a subtle movement, a shadow in the corner, caught my eye. As I turned to see who was there, the shadow waivered, then faded into the wall. I wondered if maybe I was still asleep and dreaming.

"Good Morning, young man," a deep voice from the doorway began. An older black gentleman walked into the room carrying a tray. He set the tray on a table that slid over my bed. "I'm going to sit you up here," he said as he pushed a blue button on the remote attached to the wall. My bed began to rise slowly, bringing the gray food tray into view.

"I see they put you in the Pretty Princess Room," he frowned. "That's just not right." Then he added. "My name is Stan. I've got some stuff they try to pass off as breakfast for you." He lifted the lid off the tray revealing my morning meal. "Let's see," he began. "We've got some rubber eggs. I think this object is a biscuit, be careful with that, looks dangerous. They tell

37

me this is oatmeal. You're on your own with that one.
If I were you I'd wait for mom and dad and have them
bring you in some real food."

I didn't bother to tell him that it was just mom, but
I liked Stan. I gazed at the dismal arrangement that
was my breakfast and managed to say a hoarse,
"Thanks." It was the first time I had spoken today.

"I believe your mom is in the hallway talking to the
doctor right now. They should be in to see you shortly.
Can I get you anything else?" he asked.

I shook my head.

He started to walk out but paused to gaze around
the room. "Tell you what I can do," he began, "I'll see
about getting you moved out of this room. Just not
right to put a young man in here. They ought to have a

baseball room. Lots of famous ballplayers they could put on the walls." Stan smiled at me and before I could thank him, walked out of the door.

As Stan was leaving, mom and a doctor I had not seen before walked in. She kissed my forehead and sat on the edge of my bed.

The doctor folded his arms and said, "Michael, let's talk about what happened."

Chapter 6

So it turns out I *was* clinically dead for almost ten minutes, which in dead time is not very long because, well, dead is forever. In real life time though, dead for ten minutes is pretty long. It's a pretty weird thing to be told you were dead. I couldn't help but wonder if Uncle Bob's house was heaven. If it was, then Aunt Barb's turkey ought to taste a lot better next time I go, because in the real world her turkey is all dried out and stringy. Imagine chewing on a ball of twine, not that I've done that before, but that's what it's like.

Stan made good on his promise and by the afternoon, I was moved into a plain beige room. I was definitely relieved to be out of the 'Princess Room.' It was a small comfort.

A lot of people came in and out over the next two days to check on me. Some of them asked me what it was like to be dead. I told them it's kind of like when you have a birthday. You have it, then the next day it's gone, and you go on and maybe don't remember all of it. They asked if I saw a bright tunnel or angels. I'd say, no. I saw my Uncle's barn and my dog. Most of them seemed disappointed in that, even though I told them that it was a pretty cool place.

The only thing that I didn't talk about was seeing my dad. I'm still not sure if it was him or not, but it sounded like his voice. It seems each day that goes by makes it harder to remember his voice. My dad... I haven't seen my dad in two years. He and three of his friends knew a guy who knew a guy who

won a contest to go deep-sea fishing. The guy who

won couldn't go, so he gave the prize to my dad's

friend. I remember dad was pretty excited about it.

Not because he was some big fisherman or anything,

but he was going to see two of his roommates from

college that he hadn't seen in years. He had told a lot

of stories about his college days and he told me he

would tell me even more when I got older. Anyways,

he flew to Key West, Florida to meet his friends and off

they went.

According to the news, they went out to sea on

a sunny, clear morning. A sudden storm came up in

the mid-afternoon. They radioed that they were having

engine trouble, but the weather was too bad for the

Coast Guard to respond. No one ever heard from

them again. The Coast Guard spent the next four days looking for them, but finally gave up. One year later, a judge pronounced my dad and his friends legally dead. I don't talk about it much, neither does mom, because when we do we get into a fight. I think that there's a chance he's alive out there somewhere and that maybe someday, he's going to come back home.   My mom, well she just doesn't like to talk about it.

The only thing that is worrying me now is this: if I did die, and went to Uncle Bob's house, Luther was there and Luther is dead. And, if that was my dad's voice, then maybe my dad really is dead.

Chapter 7

There was a soft knock at the door. I looked up from my iPod to see Rosie standing in the doorway. He was wearing a clean button-up shirt and his hair was combed. That meant that his mom must have made him dress up because that is not how Rosie usually looks.

"Hey!" I said. He was the first visitor that was one of my friends and I was pretty happy to see him. Rosie said a sullen "hey" and stood in the doorway looking down.

"You can come in, man." At first I wasn't sure why he was hesitating, but then I remembered, he was the one who put me here to begin with.

Rosie shuffled over and looked up and down

the length of my bed. "Can you walk?" he asked.

"Yeah, I can walk," I laughed. "I'm not dead. Well, I was dead. But yeah I can walk. I'm doing a lot better now."

Rosie let out a sigh. And then he opened up. "I was so worried, Mikey. I mean there were all these rumors that you were paralyzed and that you were dead. Every day there was another rumor worse than the one before."

"Well, I'm not paralyzed. They told me I was dead for ten minutes, but I don't remember it really." I replied.

Rosie came closer to my bed and looked me straight in the eyes. "I'm so sorry, Mikey. You are my best friend and if anything ever happened to you, especially because of me," his eyes began to tear up a little and he looked away.

"Hey Ladies!" came a familiar voice from the doorway. It was Tom. "Hate to break up this love fest, but I had to sneak up to say hi. How's it going buttheads? I think that'll be the new nickname for both of you since Rosie's butt hit your head. I kind of like it." Tom looked at me and said, "You're lucky they were able to pry your head out."

"Have some respect," said Rosie. "You're going to get us in trouble. The mean nurse said only one visitor at a time."

Tom walked into the room. "Yeah, how about that?" He wasn't a jock anymore but he still had that swagger about him. "So, how are you feeling? Did you really die?"

"Yeah, I guess," I replied. "They said I was dead for ten minutes."

"Cool," Tom started. "So that must make you a Zombie!"

Rosie changed the subject, "Do you remember anything from the pool?"

The truth was, the last thing I remember from the pool was Melissa's face as I was flying toward her. Everything else was gone. "No, not really." I said.

"Oh, Mikey," Rosie started. "After I hit you there was blood everywhere in the water. The lifeguard had to jump in. You were covered in blood. The lifeguard was covered in blood. It was terrible."

"It was so cool!" Tom exclaimed without hesitating. "It was like a shark attack. The girls were screaming. People were jumping out of the water. Do you remember the time when Bethany Parker's brother pooped in the pool and everyone scrambled to get out of the water? Well, everyone got out faster than that this time." Tom laughed, "Good times, man. Good times."

We all started laughing and talking about the poop in the pool incident when we were interrupted by a stern, angry voice.

"Gentlemen!" It was the mean nurse. She was not a very attractive woman. If I looked like that, I'd probably be mean, too. "I said one visitor at a time. Do you know what that means?"

Tom responded, "I am one visitor."

The nurse pointed to Rosie, "He makes two."

Tom turned to Rosie and pointed to his belly, "Rosie, apparently you're two visitors. I think that sounds hurtful, but rules are rules. You have to go."

And with that, the mean nurse threw them both out.

Chapter 8

I spent the next four days in the hospital undergoing tests. They do that when you almost die. The doctors said that I had a fractured neck and their concern now was nerve damage or possibly some other kind of injury.   My neck and head were still very stiff and it hurt to turn my head quickly. I was also still seeing shadows every once and while out of the corner of my eye. Otherwise, I was feeling a lot better and hoping to go home.

Just in case you're wondering, hospitals are not fun places to stay. First of all, the nurses come in at all hours of the night to wake you up to see how you're sleeping, which doesn't make any sense at all. Even if you could sleep, the beds are like cement and they put plastic covers on the mattresses and pillows that crinkle loudly every time you move, making it impossible to sleep. I think it's because they want to keep the germs off the mattress, but Tom says it's because all the old people and little kids pee the bed. Rosie says it's because people die there and dead people are disgusting. The reason for the plastic doesn't matter I guess. All I know is that it makes you really miss your own bed.

A round-faced doctor, obviously not Dr. Nosehair, came into the room as I was watching TV and my mom was reading a magazine.

"So how are we feeling?" he asked as he placed his icy hands on the back of my neck and began feeling around.

"I'm doing a lot better. I'm ready to go home."

I suggested.

"Are you still having tingling feelings any

place?" he asked slowly turning my head from side to

side. His icicle hands made me shiver. You'd think

they would know enough to warm them up a little

before touching someone.

"No, I'm doing great. Ready to go home." I

repeated.

My mom spoke up, "Tell him about the

shadows, Mikey."

I glared at her as if to say, 'What are you doing?

I want to go home!'

"It's not a big deal," I said. "It's only happened

a couple of times. I see a shadow out of the corner of my eyes every once and a while. If I turn my head it goes away. "

"Are you seeing any spots? Do you have blurred vision?" the doctor asked, as he took out a small light and began looking into my eyes. I told him I hadn't had either of those and he said "Everything looks good," as he clicked off the light. "It's probably not all that uncommon, considering the type of injury you've had. Let's keep an eye on it and let me know if it gets any worse." I laughed to myself and wondered if he knew he was making a pun when he said 'keep an eye on it.'

He stood up and cleared his throat. "Okay. I think we are ready to go home."

My heart jumped!

He pulled a clicky pen from his pocket and began writing on the charts in his hand. "I am going to restrict activity. No physical anything for a month, and no school for two weeks. No return to school until I see you at my office for a check-up. I don't want to take a chance of having you get bumped around and reinjuring yourself."

My heart sank.

Now I know most kids would be thrilled to have the first two weeks of the school year off, sort of like an extended summer vacation. But I'm not most kids. I kind of like school, especially in the beginning of the year. Everyone gets a fresh start. Everyone is wearing all of their new back-to-school clothes. The kids are nicer, the teachers are definitely nicer. You show up a couple weeks into it and everyone's cranky by then. Not to mention I'll fall behind and it's tough to catch up when you miss two weeks.

I had to try something. "But, Mom," I pleaded. "I'll fall behind. It's tough to catch up when you miss two weeks."

"I already contacted the school, Mikey. They're going to provide a tutor. She'll come to the house everyday for three hours to keep you up to speed so you don't miss anything. And Lord knows it'll be nice to have someone there part of the day while I'm at work. I won't have to worry about you being all alone."

As it turned out, I'm the one who should have

worried about being all alone.

Chapter 9

On the first official day of school, I slept in till ten o'clock. My mom came into my room and woke me to let me know that breakfast was ready. I went downstairs in my shorts and a t-shirt to my favorite, pancakes and bacon. I guess there are some advantages to almost dying.

"I have to go into work at eleven," my mom began as I was devouring the pancakes covered with melting butter and soaked in maple syrup, "but I wanted to be here when you met your tutor."

Oh! I had forgotten about that part. The only thing that could be even remotely good about having a tutor would be if she was hot, like our student teacher last year, Miss Stewart. I don't remember one thing she taught, but I really liked going to class. So did everyone else. Rosie especially had a crush on her. On her last day he brought her a flower. And then to everyone's shock, he told her he couldn't sing, but he would dance for her. Next thing you know, there's Rosie, his belly shaking, dancing in front of the whole class. We were all laughing hysterically until Miss Stewart walked over and gave Rosie a kiss on the cheek. Then we all wanted to dance for her, but it was too late.

I was chewing on bacon and picking up my second helping of pancakes when the doorbell rang. "Oh, she's here!" Mom said excitedly. She pushed her hair up and out of her eyes and stood waiting for me.

I quickly shoveled a pile of pancakes into my

mouth and followed mom, excited at the prospect of what might lie behind the door. Mom opened the door and there stood a very short, older lady with glasses, and long gray hair in a pony tail. She had a stern look about her, like she was the kind of lady you didn't want to mess with. She was someone's grandmother, only with an attitude.

"Hello," she said, in a commanding voice that could make a pit bull sit down. "I'm Mrs. Grey and I will be your tutor."

I tried to speak but I had to swallow. I tried to swallow but my mouth was full of pancakes. I realized I had no air coming in and, like in the pool, I found that I couldn't breathe. I was drowning all over again, only this time on pancakes.

"Mikey?" Mom asked. "Mikey, don't be rude. Say hi to Mrs. Grey."

I felt a surge rise from my stomach, and then a sudden cough and an explosion of half chewed pancakes flew through the air landing all over Mrs. Grey. My mom starred at me in shock. My eyes began to water. Mrs. Grey stood motionless. In the back of my mind I thought, thank God I can breathe again. And then, as I saw chunks of pancakes dribble down her hair and face, I thought this might just get me a new tutor.

Mrs. Grey spoke, "Not to worry young man. I've raised four boys and three grandchildren. While I am not accustomed to being greeted this way, this is not the first time I've been thrown-up on. I do hope, however, that you don't begin all of our sessions by spewing vomit." She brushed the pancake off her face and jacket and walked into the house.

After she cleaned up, and she and mom spoke privately for a while, mom left for work and it was just the two of us. She was a no-nonsense lady, so it was right to work. I took a bathroom break after about twenty minutes, just to get up and get out of the room. A half- hour later I tried to take another one, and that's when I got a good dose of Mrs. Grey.

"I spoke to your mother, Michael." Mrs. Grey began.

Ughh, she was calling me Michael.

"She told me that your bladder was a normal size for a boy of your age, and that she wasn't aware of any sudden bathroom urges that you had, so I don't expect you to be running off to the bathroom every twenty minutes. She also told me about your medical condition. I've tutored children who were in much worse shape than you and I had high expectations for them, which they met! I will expect the same from you. I think you'll find that I am firm and fair as long as you do what you are supposed to do."

This was going to be worse than I thought. We got back to work and it was as if time stood still. It would seem like an hour had gone by and when I looked at the clock, only five minutes had passed. I really missed school now. And then, right when I was thinking of terrible nicknames for her, she told me to put my pencil down.

"Michael, you look tired dear. Would you like to take a little break?"

She did have a heart after all. "Yeah, I am kind of tired. It seems like a lot of work to try and do all at once." She looked sympathetic, but I needed to put the icing on the cake, so I kept going. "Especially since I almost died and everything. I think this school work is really taking a lot out of me." Look tired and sad I thought to myself and let's hope she buys it.

She patted my hand. "Ahhh, there, there, dear. I think we should close these books and take a little break."

'Yes!' I thought. She bought it!

Mrs. Grey stood up and walked over to the sink and began running the water. Then she looked over at me. "Come on over. Your mother was nice enough to make you a delicious breakfast. I know it was delicious because you threw it up all over me. So the least we can do is to take care of the dishes for her." She tossed me the dish cloth. "Here you go. Let's clean!"

I think it's official. I hate Mrs. Grey!

Chapter 10

We finished the dishes. Then we swept the kitchen floor and vacuumed the living room. In addition to being my tutor, Mrs. Grey also seemed to think she was the new maid. And I was her servant boy. How did this go so horribly wrong?

I was putting the vacuum away when I saw the dark shadow out of the corner of my eye again. I stood motionless for a second, waiting to see if it would move. The shadowy figure began to sway slightly and, as I turned, it vanished. I was staring at the wall that it had disappeared through when Mrs. Grey spoke, catching me a little by surprise.

"What are you doing?" she asked with great curiosity.

In my mind I pictured Mrs. Grey as a witch and I wanted to say, "I heard your broom was in the shop so I got you a vacuum," but instead I settled on the safe answer: "I'm putting the vacuum away."

"No," she responded. "What are you doing with your head? Why are you turning your head that way?"

I explained to Mrs. Grey, "Since the accident, I sometimes see shadows out of the corner of my eye. It looks like there's a man there, but when I turn to look, it's gone. The doctor says it's normal and will go away. I'm not too worried about it." The truth was that it creeped me out every time I saw this "shadow man," as I had started to call him. It always felt like someone was there, coming closer to me, waiting for the time that I didn't look to sneak up so he could get me.

Mrs. Grey tilted her head, made a curious humming noise, and walked back to the kitchen table. She sat down and said, "Break's over."

We worked for another hour, without a pee break. Then Mrs. Grey said that she thought that would be it for the day. Those were best words I had heard since breakfast. She offered to make me a sandwich before she left and I told her no thank you, I was tired. I actually was tired after all the schoolwork and chores that I did. And yes, I was hungry too, but I didn't want Mrs. Grey in the house any longer than she had to be. Next thing you know she'd have me scrubbing toilets for my lunch.

I walked Mrs. Grey to the door and opened it for her. I'm sure she knew I couldn't wait for her to leave. This is probably why she paused on the front step and turned back toward me. She stood silent for a second, and then said that she had forgotten her purse in the kitchen. As she walked back into the house, I wanted to scream. If I had felt bad about hurling my breakfast all over her earlier, I didn't feel bad about it now. In fact, if she had made me a sandwich, I would hurl that up at her, too. Within a few seconds she was back at the door and again she paused on the front step.

"Are you sure you're alone?" she asked.

That seemed like such a weird and odd thing to ask me. "Yeah," I replied. "It's just me and my mom living here. She'll be home from work early tonight."

Mrs. Grey looked over my shoulder into the house. She nodded her head, mumbled goodbye, and walked down the sidewalk. I closed the door and even though I wasn't supposed to, I jumped in the air and shouted. "Finally, I'm alone! Free at last!"

First things first, I was going to the kitchen to get some food. And when mom came home, I would tell her how horrible Mrs. Grey was and that she would have to go. There was no way I could learn from that woman.

I rounded the corner going into the kitchen and froze in my tracks. Every drawer, every cupboard was open. I mean wide open. "Whoa!" I said aloud. I wondered how Mrs. Grey could have possibly have done that so fast and without me hearing her. I didn't think she was gone long enough from where I stood by the door to have done this. Then, out of the corner of my eye, I saw the shadow man looming. He was there watching me for the second time today. I turned quickly and he was gone.

I steeled myself and walked into the kitchen to close the drawers and cupboards. I was definitely a little freaked out as I pushed each one closed. When the last drawer was back in place, I grabbed a bag of chips and made a dash for the living room, turned on the TV and waited for mom.

Chapter 11

Mom got home around six, early by our standards. When dad was declared dead, the insurance company gave mom the money from his life insurance policy. It wasn't as much as she thought it was going to be. There was enough for funeral services and to pay off about half of the mortgage, the money we owed on the house. There was a little left over that she put into a savings account, "for a rainy day," she said. Even with that, she still had bills to pay. So mom worked part of the day at an office doing paper work and talking to customers on the phone. In the evening, and sometimes on the weekends, she worked as a waitress part-time at a diner. Some days she was home early like today. Other nights she might not be home until around ten. To do my part, I learned

71

to basically be okay by myself and not get into too much trouble.

"How did your day go, Mikey?" she asked as she kicked off her shoes and plopped down at the other end of the couch I was lying on.

"Mrs. Grey has got to go!" I said firmly. "She's a drill sergeant. She wouldn't let me use the bathroom and she made me clean the kitchen."

Mom got a big smile on her face and jumped up from the couch and ran to the kitchen. I could hear her say, "Oh my." She walked back into the living room. "Mikey, the kitchen looks wonderful, and look at this, did you vacuum in here too? I didn't even notice when I walked in." She came over and gave me a big kiss on the forehead. "Mikey, thank you so much! The house looks wonderful. You have no idea what it's like to come home after working all day and not have to do more work around here."

So much for getting rid of Mrs. Grey!

Mom made us sandwiches and we talked about our day. I even told her that Mrs. Grey opened all the cupboards and drawers before she left, but that only made mom laugh. She said I had it coming to me after I threw up my breakfast on her. I hadn't thought about that. Maybe that was Mrs. Grey's revenge? It was pretty lame, if it was.

Around seven, Rosie and Tom came over to fill me in on the first day of school. It was good to see them, especially Tom, because it was the first time since the accident that he didn't greet me with, 'Hey

Butthead.' That's not the kind of nickname you want to get stuck with.

I got all the good information. Rosie liked all of his classes except for health class with Mrs. Phelps. Rosie said she was about a hundred and thirty years old. He said when she was talking to the class she would sway back and forth like an old tree on a windy day. He kept waiting for her to fall over and crush one of the kids in the front row. Tom did not like any of his classes, and he already had homework in math and reading.

We played video games for a while and around nine, mom said it was time for them to go. As he got to the door, Rosie reached in his pocket and pulled out a folded piece of paper. "Here," he said. "This is from someone very *special*." He put an extra emphasis on the word 'special.'   The look on my face said that I wasn't sure who it could be from. Tom made a kissy face and drooled out "Melissa Burns! Duh!!"

I took the paper and quickly put it in my pocket before my mom had a chance to see it. I looked back and saw she was watching TV and not even paying attention. Good.

"Thanks, Rosie. See ya, Tom."

As they walked down the sidewalk Tom shot back, "See ya later Butthead." Rosie smacked him in the arm. I could hear him mumbling something like, "You gotta stop doing that to him..." and then their voices faded.

"I'm off to bed. Good night, Mom. Love you."

I gave my mom a kiss on the cheek. She told me to brush my teeth and that she loved me too and I went up stairs. It was a funny thing about the 'I love you.' Before dad went missing we never really said that or even hugged each other. Now, whenever one of us left for work or school or went to bed, we said it. It was like now we said those words to each other, just in case.

I crawled into bed and unfolded the note from Melissa Burns. There, in blue ink and in perfect handwriting it said:

Mike,

I hope you are feeling better.

Melissa Burns

I read it over and over, probably about twenty times. I didn't even know that she knew my name and now I get a note from her. I read it again. I folded the note back up, put it on my night stand and turned out the light. Sweet dreams, Melissa Burns.

Chapter 12

Rays of morning sunshine flooded my room, making the light-blue walls bright and reflective. I glanced at the clock; it was nine-thirty. I reached over to my nightstand to find my note, but it wasn't there. I looked on the floor around my bed and the nightstand. Still not there. I pulled the covers back and had made my way across the room to the door when I noticed the letter, sitting open on my dresser. Mom must have come in this morning to say goodbye, found my note and read it. I'm going to have to do a better job of hiding my notes from now on. Mom was usually very good about not going through my things, but I really didn't want to face a hundred questions from her about who Melissa Burns was. I picked it up, read it again, and buried it in my underwear and sock drawer.

I went downstairs and poured a bowl of cereal because, sadly, there would be no pancakes today. At exactly ten-thirty the doorbell rang and that could only mean one thing: Mrs. Grey. I opened the door but she stepped back, head tilted, waiting.

"Are you coming in?" I asked.

"That depends." she replied, "Are you going to vomit your breakfast on me this morning?"

I rolled my eyes and opened the door wider. "No."

Mrs. Grey came in and went straight to the kitchen table. She placed a large green canvas bag on the floor near her seat, and looked at me as if to ask, 'What are you waiting for?' As I settled into my chair I thought I should remind her that we were even after yesterday's prank. "You know, that was pretty impressive what you did yesterday, opening all of the drawers and cupboards in here. How did you do that so quickly? I mean, I didn't even hear a sound."

Mrs. Grey looked about the kitchen. "These were all open?"

"Yeah, very funny..." I replied.

Mrs. Grey let out a slight hum and then pulled the math text book out of her bag. "Let's start with a review of multiplying fractions."

After an hour and a half of math and science and then a quick bathroom break, we moved onto reading. Mrs. Grey pulled out two copies of a novel. Oh no, was she going to read this, too?

"Your English class started this novel yesterday so I'm afraid we're a little behind." She began. "Without giving too much away, this is a delicious murder mystery, a 'who-done-it.' If you don't mind I thought we'd read it aloud."

I tried to get out of it. "I'm kind of one of those people who read better on their own. My reading teacher last year said that it increased my comprehension doing it that way." I learned that usually anytime you said something about 'increasing comprehension' to an adult, they would be impressed.

Mrs. Grey didn't hesitate. She opened the book to the first chapter and began reading aloud. At first I was furious. I wasn't in kindergarten anymore and I didn't need some senior citizen reading to me. All I could think of was that I really could not stand this

woman. I wish I had never broken my neck. After two

pages, out of sheer boredom, I started to follow along

in the book. There was something about her voice

that drew me into the story. I didn't want to like it but

the pauses, the tone, the soothing sound made me feel

more like I was watching a movie than reading a book.

At the end of chapter three she stopped.

"What do you say we stop there for today?"

she asked. "We could use a little break."

"I don't mind reading a little more, if you want

to." I replied. "And besides, yesterday when we took a

'break,' as you called it, all we did was clean things."

Mrs. Grey closed the book and folded her

hands. Her head tilted toward me and for the first time

I saw her smile. She was probably a very pretty lady long ago.

"I know," she replied. "I probably owe you an apology. I suppose that wasn't what you had in mind yesterday, was it now? So today let's do something different. How about today we make some lunch first and then we'll attend to the chores. " And with that, she was up and making peanut butter sandwiches.

This is going to be the longest two weeks of my life.

Chapter 13

After lunch Mrs. Grey told me to go up and get my dirty clothes so she could do a load of laundry. If she was going to do laundry, then I was sure that I had more chores coming. I walked into my room and started to gather my clothes. As I turned to walk back out, I saw the note from Melissa out and open on my dresser. I had buried that in my drawer. As I stood staring at the note, I saw shadow man out of the corner of my eye in the darkened hallway. I dropped my clothes and turned quickly to look at him and, just as quickly, he was gone.

From downstairs I heard Mrs. Grey's voice, "Michael, do you need help?"

I folded the note back up and put it in my

pocket, picked up the dirty clothes and walked downstairs. Mrs. Grey put the laundry in and without a word, we started dusting the living room. After that was done, we swept and mopped the kitchen. I had given up on trying to complain and anyway, I was preoccupied wondering how my note was moving around by itself, and why I seemed to be seeing shadow man more often. After chores we got back to school work.

It pretty much went on like this for the rest of the week. Mrs. Grey found different and unusual chores for us to do. Who cleans out the fridge? And yes, there was a lot of dirt behind the toilet but, c'mon. In between bouts of chores and peanut butter sandwiches, we did school work. The only saving grace of all of this was when Mrs. Grey would read to me.

And, when I wasn't busy with all of that, I would spend the rest of my time trying to find explanations for the increasingly strange events going on. My note from Melissa hadn't moved anymore, but other strange things were happening. Lights would go on and off, the room would suddenly get really cold, little things seemed to be out of place and, along with all of this, I continued to see shadow man.

On Friday, after a few more chapters from the book, Mrs. Grey stopped reading and after a pause, looked at me. "Michael, is there something you want to tell me?"

I wasn't sure where to begin. I didn't say anything, and Mrs. Grey didn't move, waiting for an answer. After what seemed like an eternity, I finally began. "Since the accident, I haven't just been seeing shadow man. Little things have been happening that are hard to explain. Like the cupboards that day. Did you open all of the drawers and cupboards?"

Mrs. Grey leaned forward, "I was asking about your school work, Michael. Did you have something to tell me about the homework that you didn't do?"

I didn't really care about my homework right now. I pressed her again. "Did you do that to the kitchen or not?"

"No, Michael," she replied, leaning back in her chair.

We sat in silence for several minutes, Mrs. Grey folding and refolding her hands. Time seemed to stand still, both of us deep in thought, when Mrs. Grey cleared her throat. "You know, Michael, sometimes when people have died," she paused here maybe because it sounded just as weird for her to say that as it did to me to hear it, "sometimes when people die and they come back, they may have a special ability to be sensitive to," she paused again searching for the right words, "supernatural activity."

"You mean ghosts?" I asked.

"Well, something like that. Some people who have had near-death experiences have reported knowing things before they happen or being able to communicate with the deceased. Others sometimes bring back a spirit with them. It's as if a spirit in the other world attaches itself to that person to bring them back, but they aren't really back."

"How do you know all of this?" I asked.

"Oh my," she replied with confidence, "my family has had a long history with this sort of thing." She moved her chair closer to mine. "Let me ask you, do you feel threatened?"

I thought for a moment. I didn't feel threatened as much as scared and creeped out. I mean, how would you feel if things like this were happening to you? "No," I told her.

"Good, then here's what I think you should do. Sometimes if a spirit has attached itself to you, all you have to do is tell it to return."

"Wait a minute," I replied skeptically, "You mean all I have to do is tell this thing to go away and that'll be it?"

"Why yes," she replied. "Sometimes. What you need to do is to say out loud, 'Spirit, you need to return and leave me alone. Go back in peace to where you belong.'

I tried to repeat what Mrs. Grey had said but started laughing halfway through. Mrs. Grey actually laughed, too. I asked again to have her help me with the words and we made it to the end this time without too much giggling. "How do I know if it worked?" I asked.

"You'll just have to see." She replied. "Have you mentioned any of this to your mother?"

"No."

"Hummm," Mrs. Grey mused. "I don't suppose you would want to worry her; she has enough on her plate right now. Why don't we keep this to ourselves

for now?" That sounded like a good idea to me. "Tell

you what," she said, "I will stay a little longer with you

today and, before I go, I will make you a special

sandwich. No peanut butter today!"

Chapter 14

Mrs. Grey made me a bologna sandwich with a side of baby carrots before she left. So much for fine dining. I ate the bologna out of the sandwich, ignored the bread and baby carrots, and then I got some real food. I plopped on the couch with a bag of goldfish crackers, an apple and a soda. Now that's a dinner! I watched TV and devoured the goldfish until my fingers were orange and there was nothing but crumbs in the bottom of the bag. Then I dumped the crumbs into my mouth. Well, most of them made it into my mouth. One of the things I liked to do, but would never tell my friends, was to watch the Kids Network TV station. There were lots of cool shows that I used to watch that I still love. It's just that watching those shows now wasn't so cool anymore. I would get teased big time if that ever got out, so I always liked when no one was home and I could watch them by myself. It was obviously a little different being home by myself now, but I felt better because I had every light in the house on.   And so far, whatever Mrs. Grey had me do, seemed to have worked.

I had lost track of time between snacking and TV when the phone rang. It was already almost nine o'clock. It was mom.

"Hello Mikey. Did you eat? How are you feeling? Have you started your homework yet?"

How is it mom's can ask so many questions in a row without waiting for an answer? I tried to remember the order.   "I'm a little tired. I ate. Mrs. Grey made me a sandwich.   It was really good. And

I'm halfway through my homework."

"Oh good! Hopefully I'll be home before ten-thirty tonight. Don't forget to clean up your mess and please don't leave every light in the house on. Love you. Bye."

Well that wasn't so painful. I did have to get to my homework because I hadn't even looked at it yet. I left my mess in the living room, walked into the kitchen and plugged my iPod into the radio dock and started in on the stack of books on the old kitchen table. In social studies we were studying the ancient Greeks so I thought that would be a good place to start. The Greeks were cool; they had the Olympics and Gods and wars, which sounded like fun.

I was pretty focused on a story about how the

Greeks trained for battle and wasn't really paying attention to the music, until I noticed it was sounding a little staticy. I thought that was odd because, I had never heard static from the iPod before. I went back to work, but not for long. The shushing sound grew louder until it drowned out the music. Then, before I could move to check it, my soda can began to wiggle. My first thought was that it must be an earthquake, but we don't have earthquakes here in Syracuse. My soda continued to shake and, without warning, the kitchen temperature dropped until it felt like the inside of a freezer. I looked at my arm, covered with goose bumps and noticed that my breath came out in a vapor, like you'd see on a cold winter night. I sat frozen in place, too terrified to move. My soda can started to slide, shaking its way across the table.

Suddenly, the wooden chair next to me slid away from the table as if an invisible guest had pulled it out to sit down. The lights began flickering and the small light above the kitchen sink popped with a loud crack and went black. I stood up, knocking my chair to the floor. The light in the center of the kitchen cracked and went black. Next, the light above the table dimmed and popped and it too went black.

I turned from the kitchen and ran to the living room. The lamp by the door popped loudly and went out. One by one, the living room lights began cracking loudly, the sound of the static filling the room. The television glowed brightly, then exploded with light and went black. I ran for the stairs. Lights were popping and cracking all over the house and the sound of static was everywhere. The light on the stairs went

out as I reached the top step. I ran down the hall and
into my room, just as the hall lights went out. I
slammed my door shut and jumped into my bed, and
curled up in the corner. I pulled the blankets up over
my knees to my chest, and watched the two lights that
were still on.

My heart was racing. Then, as quickly as it
started, the static was gone. I could still see my breath
though and I knew that this was not over yet.
Suddenly, the ceiling light dimmed, popped and went
black, leaving only the small table lamp next to the
door barely lighting my room. The little light began to
flicker, casting long shadows. I pulled the blankets up
over my head and curled further into the corner.
Hearing the last light pop, I knew it was completely
black in my whole house. I began to shiver

uncontrollably. Then I felt a slight tug on my blanket. I

pulled back, but it tugged again, with more strength

this time. I knew I could not stop whatever was pulling

at my blanket.

Chapter 15

"Mikey?" The blanket was suddenly yanked off my head. "What in the world are you doing?" It was the first time I ever felt comforted by my mom's angry voice. "You left a mess in the living room and every light in the house is on. We're on a budget. Do you know how high the electric bill was last month? How many times do I have to tell you to help out?"

She looked so disappointed, but I was never so happy to have her home. I jumped off the bed and gave her a huge hug. She seemed a little shocked by my reaction, then she laughed a little and said, "Don't think a big hug is going to make everything okay, mister." I thought about telling her what had just happened but I was worried she would think I was crazy.

She shook her head, and then tried to avoid smiling as she said, "I brought home a couple of pieces of apple pie. Once you get your mess cleaned up we can have them for a bedtime snack."

I went downstairs to clean up my mess. She was right, all of the lights in the house were on. In the kitchen, my soda was back by my books and the chair that had mysteriously slid away from the table by itself was back in place, as if it had never been moved at all. The static that seemed to fill the whole house was replaced by music from my iPod.

After cleaning up, we had our pie and made small talk the way kids and parents do. She asked me about my day, which I said was fine, and then she told me about hers. When we finished our pie it was almost eleven, so we picked up and headed upstairs and said goodnight.

As I sat on my bed, lights on, too scared to sleep, I couldn't help thinking about everything that had happened tonight. So much for Mrs. Grey's 'just go away advice' I thought. Her words from the afternoon echoed in my mind. For over an hour I tried to convince myself that I was safe but there was no escaping the facts of what had happened. I was actually afraid. So, for the first time since my dad went missing, I walked down the hall and knocked gently on her door.

"Mom, I had a bad dream," I whispered into the darkness of her room.

She sleepily pulled the covers back so I could get in. I felt safer with her being there, but part of me believed that whatever this thing was that was haunting me, if it wanted to, could get me anywhere.

Chapter 16

The rest of the weekend went by as smoothly as it could, considering that I was being haunted. There were no major events like Friday night, but there were a lot of little things and some creepy feelings. The lights sometimes would dim a little, like during a power surge, and the small temperature drops happened a couple of times, but my imagination was the worst of it. I was starting to think that everything that happened around the house was because of the spirit. I mean, my mom is always misplacing her keys or her sunglasses, but now when she asked if I had seen them, I was wondering if someone...or something had moved them. It was making me more than a little paranoid. The worst part of all, though, was that I hadn't seen shadow man all weekend. Honestly, that scared me more than anything. Where was he and why wasn't I seeing him?

I met Mrs. Grey at the door on Monday morning.

"Well," I started, standing in the doorway, my hands on my hips, "your 'just go away' advice was a colossal failure." After she asked me if I planned on letting her in or just standing there all morning, I moved aside and we headed for the kitchen. I explained everything that had happened. She sat and listened, humming once and a while. "So what do I do now?"

"Well, obviously this spirit wants something. It's possible it doesn't realize that it is dead, but from what you are describing, it sounds like it wants to get

THEY CALL ME ZOMBIE

your attention." She hummed some more. "I think if you truly want to find out the answer, you need to ask it what it wants."

I stared at her in shock. "You want me to ask this thing what it wants? Are you crazy?"

"It's the only way to find an answer," she replied calmly.

"That's exactly the problem," I growled. "I don't want it to answer. It's easy for you to say ask it what it wants, but I'm the one who has to deal with it."

Mrs. Grey leaned forward and looked me in the eye. "If you want to stop being frightened, Michael, you have to face your fears."

I hated that she was making sense. As much as

I was terrified by what I had to do, I knew she was right. I began to get a sick feeling in the pit of my stomach. It reminded me of when I was a kid and I had to go to the doctor's to get a shot. You knew it was going to hurt but you had to do it anyway. "So, how do I do this?" I mumbled reluctantly.

Mrs. Grey shifted in her chair, looked at me directly and in a calm, whispery voice replied, "You simply ask it what it wants."

I didn't have to ask Mrs. Grey how I would know if it worked. Based on what I saw after the last time, I was sure I would know when my answer came.

Chapter 17

After Mrs. Grey left for the afternoon, I went to the kitchen and sat in my chair. Even though strange events were happening all over the house, the kitchen seemed to have been the starting place for several of them. I placed my hands flat on the table and spoke, "Whatever you are, please tell me what you want." There was no response so I tried again, nervous and unsure of what to expect. "If you can hear me, give me a sign." Nothing. "Give me sign if you can hear me."

I heard a shuffling sound and felt the hair on my arm begin to rise. "Can you hear me?" I repeated.

"Yes," came a raspy, whispering reply.

My hands began to tremble. I don't think I had ever been so scared, but Mrs. Grey was right: I needed to face my fears. "What do you want?"

"I want you...," the whispering began. "I want you to...," there was a long pause. "I want you to dance the hokey pokey." Then there was a sudden explosion of laughter.

Tom and Rosie came falling through the kitchen door, laughing hysterically. Tom fell to the floor and Rosie sat down next to me in the chair that had moved by itself.

"What were you doing?" Rosie asked, still laughing.

"Nothing," I responded, embarrassed by being caught and by what I was doing. "What are you guys doing here, and haven't you ever heard of knocking before you come in?"

Tom sat up on the kitchen floor. "The door was open, Butthead. Who were you talking to?"

I didn't know how much they had heard, but a plan to cover myself quickly came to mind. I pulled my cell phone from my pocket. "I was talking to my mom," I lied, showing them the phone. "We must have gotten cut off."

"You didn't sound like you were talking to your mom." Tom commented.

"I'm not really a big fan of the nickname Butthead," I said to Tom, trying to change the subject.

"Yeah," said Rosie, coming to my defense, "I told you to stop calling him that."

"Zombie it is then," Tom laughed.

Rosie stood up and pulled a note from his pocket and slapped it down on the table. "It's another note from Melissa." he said, sliding it over to me. "You better write her back this time, Mikey. She asked if I had a note back from you and she didn't look happy when I told her no. Seriously man, you don't not write back to Melissa Burns. She's way too nice and..."

"And she's a hottie," Tom interrupted in a high-pitched voice.

Rosie shot Tom a look of exasperation. Tom was always interrupting. Rosie continued, "Yes, and too good-looking to not write her back. You've got to get going on this."

Even though Rosie had used the word 'seriously,' I knew he was right. I opened the note and read it.

Tom was quickly off the floor trying to look over my shoulder as I folded the note back up. "Come on, Mikey, let me see it."

"No."

Tom continued to press me about the note, but fortunately Rosie interceded. "Leave him alone, Tom, this is love. You can't interfere with affairs of the heart. Seriously."

Tom and I both looked at Rosie because he had sounded like a Hallmark greeting card. And we both started to laugh. I grabbed a pen and a sheet of paper and scribbled a quick note back to Melissa and gave it to Rosie.

Rosie and Tom stayed until seven, when my mom got home. Because she was home early and happy to see my friends, she took us all out for ice cream. We

laughed and had fun. It was a welcome relief from

Mrs. Grey and whatever was hanging around my

house. And I had a new note from the girl of my

dreams. Despite everything that had been going on,

this turned out to be a pretty good day.

Chapter 18

I woke up Tuesday morning feeling pretty good. Since I had last tried to communicate with whatever had followed me back from the dead, nothing new had happened. Mom had left for work and Mrs. Grey would be here in an hour. Plus, it was morning and nothing usually happened in the mornings. It seems like things are always scarier at night, when it's dark.

I had breakfast and decided to take a shower before Mrs. Grey arrived. Getting out of the shower, rolling clouds of steam filled the room and I realized I had forgotten to turn on the bathroom fan. I flipped the fan switch and wiped the mirror with my towel so I could see myself.

As I was bent over and brushing my teeth, I began to remember how in almost every scary movie I had seen, the main character looks into a mirror and there behind them is a ghost or monster or something. Even though you know it's coming, it's still scary. I hesitated to look in the mirror now. What if there was something there?

This was stupid. Now I was just scaring myself. I decided to face my fears and slowly raised my head. The only scary thing I saw was my messy hair. I dipped my head back down and quickly raised it up to the mirror again. Still nothing there. Ha! I laughed at the silliness of it. I stepped to the right, and then looked back. Still nothing. I stuck out my tongue and made a face. Now it became a game of me moving left, right and down, peeking looks into the mirror. The only thing to see was me making one goofy face after another.

After I got bored of that game, I gelled my hair and opened the bathroom door.

'Ahhhh!" I screamed, as I fell backward with a crashing thud onto the bathroom floor. Standing directly in the doorway was a man. He was there, but he wasn't there. His skin was almost clear, but not so that I could see through him. He looked thin, but had a muscular build. Even though his skin seemed milky-white, his hair was clearly red and his eyes were black, like shark eyes. They were glaring right at me. My heart jumped into my throat.

He moved closer and his hands moved slowly from his waist, out and up to his side, as if he wanted to lean with both hands against the doorway. "No, No, No!" I screamed, feet pumping, pushing my body back against the far wall of the bathroom getting as far away as I could. His chest seemed to expand as if he had taken in a great breath and his head tilted sideways, eyes still staring. Then, the image moved back, became blurry and was gone. I sat shaking on the floor for I don't know how long. My skin was covered in goose bumps, which made me realize that the temperature had dropped about thirty degrees. Slowly, I began to understand, that I had seen a ghost. Now I knew what had come back with me from the dead. And it was the most frightening thing I had ever seen.

Chapter 19

I dashed from the bathroom to my room, grabbed some clothes, and sprinted downstairs to get dressed. When Mrs. Grey arrived, we sat at the kitchen table and I told her what had happened in every detail. She listened intently, humming every once in a while the way she does.

"Well," she began. "That sounds so terrifying."

"Yeah, it was!" I replied thinking that was the understatement of the year.

"Well, since you had the opportunity to ask it what it wants, did you?"

"What?" I answered, completely in shock.

"Why didn't you ask it what it wants?" she

calmly repeated.

"Oh, I don't know," I began, as I felt the blood flowing to my face in anger. "I'm half- naked walking out of my bathroom and a creepy red-haired ghost is standing there looking like he wants to kill me. I suppose, as I was struggling to keep my towel up while I was sliding across the floor, I should have said, 'Hey Mr. Creepy Ghost Man with the shark death-eyes, can I get you something?'"

Mrs. Grey, put off by my sarcasm, sat back in her chair and folded her arms, "Well, it just seems to me that you had the perfect opportunity to ask this spirit why it's here," she said softly.

"I don't think he had to use the bathroom," I continued, still angry. "I mean, we have two other perfectly good bathrooms, he could have used one of them. Now I may never be able to go again. I'm going to worry that the ghost is waiting outside every time I close the bathroom door. Do you know what kind of pressure that is?"

Mrs. Grey smiled politely. "I suppose you're right."

We sat in stony silence for several minutes. My anger began to subside and fear crept back into my thoughts. "What do I do now?" I half-whispered.

"I have some thoughts on the matter," Mrs. Grey began. "I spoke to my grandmother last night and she offered some advice."

"You mean your mother," I said quickly.

"Oh my, no, both of my parents passed when I was young. My grandmother raised me for a time and she is still quite alive. One hundred and two next week," she said with a smile of pride on her face.

I began to do the calculations in my head. If Mrs. Grey was a grandmother then that meant that those kids also had a great, great grandmother or was it a great, great, great grandmother? I began to get confused.

Mrs. Grey went on, "My grandmother said that spirits who return use a great deal of energy to communicate and that, like us, they need to rest. That would explain why there have been days without incident after some of the major events you've told me about. So, because this spirit showed himself to you today, we can assume that it may be a day or two before you have to worry about another visitation."

"Did your grandmother say what I should do when it comes back?" I asked, relieved that I may have a break for a couple of days.

"Yes," she smiled. "You need to ask it what it wants."

Great! I thought. I was right back where I started.

Chapter 20

Mrs. Grey and I put schoolwork aside for the day and focused on what was going on. She told me more about her grandmother. Her name was Mabel, and while she was giving birth to Mrs. Grey's mom, she had a near death experience. The doctor was able to revive her and though she didn't have a ghost come back with her, she saw and heard strange things. She described seeing a tunnel with a bright light and told of people whom she knew were dead standing around her. She described it all as very peaceful. When some time had passed, she began to see visions and some of these would talk to her. Other visions did not talk, so they would point or sometimes move things. Still others would simply appear and disappear for no apparent reason.

"You have to remember," Mrs. Grey said wistfully, "people are often afraid of what they don't understand. And so it was that when people in the town heard rumors about the visions, they began to think that my grandmother was crazy. They put her in a mental asylum and locked her away for twenty years. Twenty years." Mrs. Grey gently folded and unfolded her hands.

"How did she get out?" I asked. "Did the visions go away?"

"Oh my, no," she said. "She simply stopped talking about them. After a few years the doctors decided she was better and able to leave. She went home, but there wasn't at all much to go home to. Her children had all grown up and left, and the town, like many towns hit by the Depression, was just a shell of

what it had been."

"How did...," I started to ask a question, then

thought that maybe I shouldn't.

Mrs. Grey understood. "You want to know how

I came to live with my grandmother." She smiled at

me. "My mother and father were killed in a train

accident when I was five. Having no other living

relatives, the state sent me to live with my

grandmother. As I was growing up she would tell me

about her visions. She would know who was calling

when the phone rang; sometimes she knew when an

accident might happen or even when a person might

die. She told me that the visions would tell her."

"Did you ever see any of them?"

"No, Michael, I don't have the Gift."

"The Gift?" I asked, shocked that she made this sound like something good. "It's not a gift, Mrs. Grey. I spend every day worrying and waiting for something to happen. Every time there is a noise or a knock in the house I think something's happening again. I'm scared to death. It's not a gift." I corrected her.

Mrs. Grey reached out and held my hand. "Michael, sometimes we have burdens placed upon us and we don't understand why. For whatever reason, you seem to have an ability that so few people have. And like those people in the town where my grandmother lived, you fear it because you don't understand it. Sometimes, Michael, what we think is a burden turns out to be a gift."

I know she was trying to comfort me, but all it did was bring tears to my eyes.   "Will you stay until my mom gets home?" I asked.

"That I will, Michael."

Chapter 21

Mrs. Grey stayed until 7:30, when my mom got home. She explained to mom that we had been working on a project. After Mrs. Grey left, mom and I ate, talked very little, watched her shows, and then went to bed. Knowing that whatever was haunting me had probably used up a lot of its energy and that I'd probably be safe tonight brought little comfort. The fact remained that I would have to face this thing again, but I didn't know when or where.

Nothing happened over the next two days, which only added to the tension. Every creak, every little noise, every imagined movement brought with it the fear that I was about to be visited again. I continued to hope that maybe Mrs. Grey or her grandmother might have an answer for me. Then, on Friday morning Mrs. Grey arrived with a small white cardboard box tied with a string.

"I brought something special for you," she said, as she set it on the table.

I wondered what could be inside. Maybe some special family pendant or amulet that would protect me from whatever was haunting me. The box felt heavy in my hands and I struggled to untie the string. Finally I slid the string off to the side and opened the box. Inside were two flaky golden-crusted pastries. I sat back and looked at Mrs. Grey with a puzzled expression.

"It's our last day together, Michael," she began. "I thought we would celebrate with turnovers. I hope you like apple."

With all that had been going on, I actually forgot that Monday I would head back to school. In a way I felt relieved. I was sure that school would be much safer than being home alone all day. I mean, what kind of a ghost goes to school to haunt you? On the other hand, that also meant that I wouldn't be seeing Mrs. Grey anymore. I gazed down at the pastries with a strange and unexpected feeling of disappointment.

Mrs. Grey got some plates and we ate our turnovers. She finished reading the story that we had started last week and we quietly worked on math and science. And then she began to pack her bag to leave. "You know, Michael, I must say that I have enjoyed our time together."

"That's it?" I asked. "You're just leaving?"

"Well, that's how it works, dear. I tutor you for two weeks and then my employment is up and I move on."

"What about the ghost?" I pleaded. "What if I need help?"

Mrs. Grey handed me a slip of paper. "Here is my cell phone number, Michael. You can call me anytime you want." She paused and smiled sweetly at me. "You are a very dear young man, Michael. I will be available anytime you need me. Just call."

"What about the ghost?" I asked again. "I know I have to talk to that thing again. Can you stay and we can do it together? We can try it right now." I said,

hearing the desperation in my own voice.

Mrs. Grey placed her hand under my chin and

lifted my head up gently. "Michael, whatever came

back with you wants to talk to *you*. I know this is

difficult, but you'll have to do this alone." She stepped

close, gave me a quick hug and walked to the door.

She paused at the door and scanned the room one last

time, then looked back at me. "Good luck, Michael."

And with that, she was gone, and I was left

alone in the house, waiting for the inevitable.

Chapter 22

As I stood in the doorway and watched Mrs. Grey drive off, I felt the need to get out of the house. I slipped into my old red sneakers without tying the laces and went outside. It was a sunny and warm September day and if I could spend part of it outside, more importantly avoiding the inside, I would. I walked over to the neighbor's backyard and sat on their swing set, wondering what I should do. I could go back in and try to talk to whatever it was. It was a no-brainer that I'd rather see that thing during the day than at night. Maybe if I called to it, it would show up now, while it was light out. It wasn't a good plan, but it was a plan.

Looking at the house, I took a deep breath and

walked slowly back toward the door. I was wondering if I should just go in and sit in the middle of the couch, which was in the middle of our well-lit living room, and call to it. Then I wondered if I should maybe sit on one side of the couch just in case it wanted to sit down. Maybe I should stand by the wall so it couldn't sneak up on me? Whatever I was going to do, I decided it would be in the living room where the big windows provided the most light. For some reason, this gave me confidence.

I walked back into the house and was immediately struck by the frigid temperature. The confidence I had outside evaporated instantly and I knew that it was waiting for me. I went to the center of the living room, but before I could speak, I heard the creaking of our cellar steps from behind the door just off the kitchen. The basement steps always creaked when someone walked on them and since I knew I was alone, that could only mean one thing. I walked cautiously toward the cellar door, the temperature getting colder the closer I got. I placed a shaky hand on the freezing door knob, turned it and pulled it slowly open.

There was nothing but darkness down in the basement and, as I stared into the blackness, I heard the barely visible bottom step creak loudly. That was it. I stepped back and yelled downstairs. "Hey, I am not going down there!"

I slammed the door closed and went back to the living room mumbling to myself and maybe to the ghost as I went. "I am not going down there. I'm supposed to ask what you want, and I'm asking, but I do not have to do it in the basement! No way! No way!"

I went back to the middle of the living room and yelled, my words coming out in frozen mist, "If you want to talk we're talking up here. I am NOT going down there!" I stopped surprised by my defiance. Then I began to worry, what if I made it mad?

The sound of an exhale of breath, like a heavy sigh, came from the kitchen and I turned quickly, looking toward the empty room. Almost as suddenly, I sensed the unmistakable feeling of fear rising, just like the last time I saw it. And making matters even worse, I somehow knew that it wasn't in the kitchen, but right behind me. I slowly pivoted and there it stood in the hallway, just beyond the steps leading upstairs. The vision was clearer than last time. His hair was definitely red and he appeared to be wearing a white t-shirt and dark pants. His muscular arms seemed as white as his shirt, yet somehow I could tell them apart. The vision rocked from side to side and then from front to back in dreamy slow motion. At first he seemed lost, as if he were looking for something he could not find. And then his black eyes came to rest directly on mine. They swelled as if he recognized me and his mouth opened in a silent scream. I felt my arms begin to tremble uncontrollably. I wanted to run but I was literally frozen with fear.

"What do you want?" I heard my shaky and frightened voice ask.

The entity's eyes grew wider and it sank downward, falling to its ghostly knees. His hands opened and came up to his side as if it were pleading for something. His face contorted in a painful expression, the muscles in his neck straining, and in a deep, hushed tone I heard it whisper, "Help me."

Chapter 23

My whole body was shaking as I watched the ghostly vision beg for my help. Still too terrified to move, I asked again, "What do you want from me?"

The ghost tilted its head back, mouth open and eyes narrowed, clearly frustrated with me. Then, in one fluid motion, its head came back down, and it rose up and leaned forward. His black eyes grew large and fixated on mine once more. His expression had gone from a look of pain to one of pure anger and in a much more forcefully hushed tone, his face now snarling, he growled his command. "Help Me!"

"Leave me alone!" I yelled, as I felt myself turning and fleeing toward the front door. As I approached it, the door suddenly slammed shut. I turned back and the ghost, still there, fought as if he was trying to break free of invisible chains holding him down.

"Aggghhhh!" I heard it howl as it twisted and turned, the sound echoing in a roar throughout the house. His unearthly eruption triggered a series of booming explosions as every open door in the house slammed shut.

I don't know how it happened but somehow the fear inside me turned to anger. With fists clenched and jaw tight, I stepped closer to the ghostly image and yelled, "How am I supposed to help you?!"

Suddenly, the ghost stopped struggling and floated backward, a look of relief on its face. His black eyes grew smaller, closed, and then opened to me once more. He nodded his head and disappeared like

fog before my eyes.

"Holy crap!" I screamed and ran for the door. I

fumbled with the handle, yanked it open and bolted

into the front yard. I fell to my knees, my chest

heaving up and down as I struggled to catch my breath.

The sudden warmth of the fall day was a welcome

relief from the frigid house.

"I just talked to a ghost! Oh my God, I just

talked to a ghost!" I couldn't stop repeating it to

myself. I was frightened and exhilarated all at the

same time, but mostly frightened. My hands shaking, I

reached into my pocket for my cell phone and dialed

Mrs. Grey's number.

Chapter 24

She answered on the third ring.

"It was here!" I yelled into the phone. "I just talked to the ghost! It was the scariest thing I've ever done in my life!" Mrs. Grey kept trying to ask questions and I just kept yelling the same thing back to her. "I just talked to the ghost! It was the scariest thing I've ever done in my life!"

After what seemed like an hour of repeating myself as I paced frantically around the yard, Mrs. Grey calmed me down. I did the best I could to collect my thoughts and tried to explain everything that had happened in exact detail. It wasn't easy because, every time I would start talking about it, I would get worked up all over again.

"Well," Mrs. Grey began, after I had finished. "That certainly didn't take very long for the spirit to communicate with you. I suppose that means that it has something important it needs your help with."

"It's a ghost!" I replied. "It's dead! Who knows for how long? How important can it be? Why does it have to come barging into my life for help?"

"Oh, I'm sure we can't say why it's chosen you, but it's clear that you have some work to do if you want this spirit to leave you alone."

I groaned at the thought of another possible encounter. "I still don't know what it wants," I began in frustration. "I asked it what it wanted and it didn't say. I'm pretty sure I did my part here." The image of the ghostly vision's angry gaze flashed in my mind.

"You don't understand Mrs. Grey, this thing is…, is…," I stumbled over my words unable to finish.

There was a pause and I heard Mrs. Grey hum the way she often does. "Michael, it seems to me that you're missing a couple of very important and obvious facts. First of all, the spirit appears to desperately need your assistance, which would seem to give you some power in this situation. It asked for your help. Secondly, when you told the spirit that you wouldn't go downstairs, it appeared upstairs. When you yelled to the spirit, asking it how you could help, it retreated and went away."

Mrs. Grey was somehow making sense again, but I didn't like it.

"Michael, even though this apparition is

frightful to you, *you* are the one in control. You've proven that today. You'll need to remember that the next time you talk to it."

The *next* time I talk to it? First of all, I wouldn't exactly call today a conversation and, like the ghost, I had used up a lot of energy. Unlike the ghost, I used all of my energy trying not to pass out from fright. I was suddenly exhausted. "Mrs. Grey, I really wish you were the one doing all the talking to the ghost."

"Oh my," she replied, "I'm afraid I'd be scared to death to talk to a ghost."

Chapter 25

Knowing that the ghost would need to rest and that I was safe for at least a little while, I had a pretty normal weekend. Mom took me back-to-school shopping at the mall on Saturday and, even though I would almost rather be haunted by a ghost than go shopping, it wasn't all that bad. It only took about an hour and a half for me to get what I needed. It would have taken a lot less time if mom hadn't made me try on everything. Not only did she make me try on the clothes, after I came out to show her, she would be off looking for more clothes for me. Every time I came out of the dressing room it was like a game of hide and seek. I spent half of the time walking around in new clothes just looking for her.

When the agony of shopping was finally over,

we stopped to eat lunch. I had a huge greasy

cheeseburger and fries. After I devoured that, mom

said she needed to do some shopping of her own and

released me to the freedom of the mall. There were

plenty of stores I could have gone to, but I immediately

headed to the bookstore. I wandered around a few

aisles until I found the section labeled 'Supernatural.'

There was book after book about ghosts and spirits.

There was another huge section about vampires and

werewolves and I thought that was pretty dumb. I

mean, just because there was a popular teen movie

out about these ghouls, didn't mean they were real. I

was looking back at the ghost section when it occurred

to me that two weeks ago, I would have thought

ghosts were dumb, too. Now I have one of my very

own scaring me every couple of days.

I searched through several of the books. None of them offered any advice on what to do if you bring a ghost back with you from the dead. I decided that if I survived this whole ordeal, I might have to be the first to write a book about it. I walked down the row of books imagining myself as a famous writer and it was pretty cool. I would have book signings and people would want my autograph. I'd probably get to be on TV shows and then they'd make my book into a movie and I would get to meet famous Hollywood stars. As I rounded the corner of the aisle, deep in my fantasy, I suddenly found myself face to face with Melissa Burns.

I felt my face contort into a look of stupid shock and surprise while Melissa simply and gracefully flipped her hair back and in a dreamy voice said, "Hi, Mikey."

Try not to sound stupid, I thought to myself. The silence between us was growing longer as I was thinking of what to say. Just when I decided that, 'Hey Melissa, how's it going?' would be a good start, I suddenly blurted out, "I'm just here looking for a book. I like to read. I like to read books. I like good books to read. I was just looking for a good book to read, here in the bookstore."

There it was. I had managed to sound like a mindless dweeb. I don't know if it was bad luck or just fate, but I was never good at speaking to girls. Rosie could charm a girl all day and Tom was a funny guy who made them laugh. Me, I was a babbling idiot every time a girl said hi to me.

Melissa just smiled politely. "Are you coming back to school soon?"

"Yeah, I come back Monday. I can't wait. I was so bored at home." First I was babbling, now I was lying.

Melissa smiled, "Did you get my last note?"

I was just about to answer when fate decided it had to kick me one more time. From over my shoulder came the all too familiar voice of my mom. "Mikey, who is your friend?"

Before I could even say a word, my mom stepped in front of me and did what moms have probably done since the beginning of time; find ways to embarrass their children.

"Oh my goodness, aren't you a beautiful girl."
She began. "Mikey, how come you've never told me
about her? Look at her, she's so gorgeous. Mikey's
going back to school on Monday, you should come
over to the house someday after school."

I want you to think of the brightest shade of red
you can think of, and then multiply it by one hundred.
My face was another hundred times brighter than that.
I was mortified. Before my mom could began
bombarding her with questions, I managed to pull her
away, say a quick goodbye to Melissa and get out of
the mall. Someone who was dead should not have to
suffer this type of embarrassment!

Chapter 26

Monday morning. Back to school. It was good to be back. I missed the hustle and noise of the busy morning hallways. Lots of kids were stopping to say hi, not that I was really popular or anything, but I think kids wanted to say hi to someone who was dead just a few weeks ago. It gave them something to talk about. When their parents asked, 'What did you do in school today?' they could tell them they talked to a dead kid.

There were also pockets of kids I didn't know. As I walked past them down the crowded halls I could hear their hushed voices saying, "That's the kid who died." And "There goes the zombie." One or two times kids actually shouted "zombie" out loud but I couldn't tell who it was or where it came from. Other kids just stood and stared as I walked by and that was okay too.

I managed to find my way to my locker and then to morning classes and the teachers were pretty decent about telling me to ease back into school. It didn't hurt that I had all of my work caught up, thanks to Mrs. Grey.

The morning classes went well and before I knew it, it was time for lunch. I stopped at my locker to drop off my books, looking forward to lunch, but not the food part. First of all, lunch is a social event. It's time to hang out with your friends and have fun. Secondly, I, like many of my friends, had given up long ago on the cafeteria providing any type of edible food. I mean the food all sounds great; pizza, tacos, French fries. I love all of that, just not when it comes from the

school. Every kid out there knows exactly what I mean.
As I closed my locker door, there was Melissa Burns
standing right next to me. This was the second time
now that she had suddenly appeared. She smelled
wonderful!

"Hi, Mikey," she said, as she leaned against the
lockers.

'Oh boy,' I thought. I took a deep breath and
tried to be cool.

"Hey, Melissa," I was off to a great start. "Sorry
about the bookstore and my mom the other day. She's
a nerd." Did I just call my mom a nerd? Who calls
their mom a nerd?

"That's okay," Melissa replied. "I thought she
was very sweet. Listen, I was wondering if you wanted

to walk home together after school?"

I swallowed hard. "Uh, yeah. Sure."

"Great," she replied, popping off the locker with a big smile. "Meet me by the gym after school."

And with that, she turned, her hair flowing gently and walked down the hallway, her sweet scent still lingering near me. I thought I must be dreaming. I stood and watched as she floated away.

"Ah, nothing makes my heart soar like young love." Rosie had come up from behind me.

"It makes me want to puke." Tom was there, too.

"Welcome back, Mikey," Rosie said. "Come on, let's go to lunch, and you can tell me all about it."

Tom made a sickening face, "Great! Mikey's romance and school lunch? I'll definitely puke now."

Chapter 27

Hanging out in the cafeteria was fun. I told Rosie and Tom all about my conversation with Melissa. Rosie was pretty happy for me. Tom couldn't understand why a girl like Melissa would be interested in, as he put it, 'a once-dead-zombie-dork,' like me. It felt great being back to school.

Before I knew it, the lunch bell rang and I had just enough time to use the bathroom before my next class. I hustled down the hallway and pushed open the heavy wooden door to the boy's bathroom. I had only taken three steps in when I noticed that my breath formed into a frozen mist, like I had just walked out into a winter morning. I had completely forgotten about my ghost since coming back to school. I figured that, since the only place I had seen or felt him was at home, that's where he'd stay. I figured wrong.

I stood in the center of the room and turned slowly waiting for him to appear. It took only seconds. He stood by the door I had entered, blocking my escape. He was dressed the same as the last time I had seen him and had the same moment of unawareness, as if he were lost. Then his black eyes came to rest on me and it was clear he'd found what he was looking for. His eyes narrowed and he pointed toward the door and said something I could not hear. My pulse was racing. It was just as scary seeing him in school as it was at home. Here I was in a building full of hundreds of people, yet somehow he found me alone.

He gestured again toward the door, more

forcefully this time. I raised my hands and shrugged, unsure what he was trying to tell me. His facial features made it look like he was screaming mad, but what came out in a very low whispery voice was one muffled word: "Out!"

I stood motionless. Suddenly the door burst open in front of the ghost and in walked Brenda's evil brother, Craig, and two of his sidekicks.

"Hey," Craig began as the door closed. I stood looking over his shoulder, and saw that the ghost had vanished. "What's up Butthead?"

I wondered at first if Tom had told him that unflattering nickname, but I suspected that Craig, being a bully, would have thought of that all on his own.

THEY CALL ME ZOMBIE

"Hey guys, this is the kid from the pool who got his head squashed by the chunky kid." Craig walked forward and looked me over. I felt like I was standing before a wolf who was sizing up his meal before attacking. "So," Craig continued standing just inches from my face. "I heard you were dead."

His breath smelled. What did he have for lunch, dog poop?

"Yeah, I was for a little bit." I said, slowly stepping away from the dog poop breath.

Suddenly Craig poked me in the chest with his finger. I was startled and surprised by how much his finger poke hurt. "Listen," he began again, a menacing scowl across his face, "I don't like dead people." His two idiot friends laughed. Craig started to circle me slowly and I turned to stay face-to-face with him. "I also don't like zombies," he added. "That's what they're calling you, right Zombie?"

"He hates zombies," chimed in one of the two goons who were behind me now.

Craig stopped and leaned in again. "If I see you in here again, you're going to wish you were dead because I'll smash your brains in just like they do to zombies in the movies."

I didn't want to show any weakness, but I rubbed the aching spot where he had poked me. It was a total attack on my senses. His dog poop breath was clogging my respiratory system and his finger poke of steel was damaging my soft tissue. "Can I go?" I asked.

"One more thing," he said poking me on the other side of my chest which seemed to hurt as much as the first. "If I see you talking to Melissa Burns again, I will kill you."

Craig nodded his head for me to go and I turned and walked in between his two hulking friends toward the door. I pulled at the heavy door as the throbbing pain in my chest continued. I shuffled down the hallway in a daze and in pain. In just a few brief minutes I had been haunted and bullied and I was not a big fan of either one.

Chapter 28

I had barely enough time to make it to social studies class. As I weaved through the crowded hallway still feeling the effects of the second finger poke of steel, I thought back to the bathroom. The ghost said, 'out,' and he pointed to the door. Why would he do that? It almost seemed like he was trying to warn me. I kept replaying the scene over and over in my mind, unsure of what to make of what had happened. If he really wanted to help me he could have just appeared and scared the crap out of Craig and his Neanderthal friends. It certainly would have saved me some pain.

I walked into the classroom and Mrs. Perkins, the social studies teacher said hi and asked how I was doing. She pointed out my seat, told me to come up to her desk after she got the class started. She then told the kids to get with their partner and get going. I watched as several of the pairs headed for the computers and some of the other partners left for the library. Within a couple of minutes she motioned for me to come up.

"So," she began, "I see you've done a good job with keeping up with your assignments. At home you've been studying about the Greeks. When you read about the Greeks and, particularly, the culture of the Athenians, what did you discover?" She answered her own question. "I'm sure you discovered that the Greeks were very interested in their community. So, based on that, we are doing research projects on our community. Last Friday, the students chose a partner and a community research assignment. Since you weren't here, your partner and assignment have already been chosen." Mrs. Perkins nodded toward the back of the classroom and said, "You'll be working with Liz."

My eyes followed Mrs. Perkin's nod to the second shortest girl in the sixth grade, Liz Lorman. I didn't really know much about Liz. I knew she was short and that was about it. I don't remember seeing her hang out with friends or play any sports. I think I might have seen her in band during a concert in the gym last spring but I couldn't be sure. I was also pretty sure that she was smart though. I know her name was always on the list for awards at the end of the quarter so she must get good grades. I grabbed my books and headed down the aisle to the short, red haired girl sitting slouched in her seat with her arms crossed. I was going to be working with an elf, an angry elf from the looks of it.

I set my books down and said, "Hi. I'm Mike. I guess we're working together."

The most interesting thing happened next. Liz sat up and her face lit up with the most amazing smile. It transformed her from what I thought was just a shy, short kid into a very cute girl with confidence. "Hi, I'm Liz."

The funny thing about it was that, in an instant, it felt like Liz was someone I had known for a very long time. There was no other way to explain it.

"So," she said, as I sat down next to her, "do you want to hear about the project?"

Chapter 29

Liz looked off into the distance for a second in a way that clearly suggested she was organizing her thoughts and then she turned back to me. "Mrs. Perkins wants us to show an interest in our community, like the Greeks did with theirs. So, she's having us do a research project on something historic in our community. The project can be a written report or research paper. We can interview people or make a model of something, so we have a lot of choices. Each pair had a partner go up and pull a topic out of a hat."

Liz went on describing some of the various topics that other students had selected at random. To be honest, I had a hard time concentrating. She was so enthusiastic and outgoing and cute, I think I was still stunned that I had never noticed her before. As she continued on, I noticed that below her red curls, she had the most amazing green eyes I had ever seen. I actually couldn't even think of anyone I knew with green eyes. Her eyes seemed to come alive as she spoke. I was no longer paying attention. In fact by this point, I couldn't even hear what she was saying anymore; it was like I was in a trace.

"What are you doing?" Liz leaned forward, her red curls dangling in front of her eyes. "Mike, what are you doing? Are you okay?"

I snapped out of my dream-like daze. "Oh, I was just thinking about what you said," I lied, trying to cover up the fact that she caught me staring at her. Now I should have just stopped there, but not me, I had to add more. "I was thinking about what you said and it was interesting and I really like it." Liz looked confused so, naturally, I babbled on. "It was kind of interesting the part you mentioned before. I liked that part and I was still thinking about how interesting and how much I like it because it was interesting,"

Liz folded her arms as I had first seen her and slouched back into her seat. I'm pretty sure she was thinking of telling me to take a hike and that she'd rather do the project alone. She just had that angry-elf look going again and I knew I had to do something fast.

"Look," I said leaning forward to whisper so that others couldn't hear me. "I was looking at your eyes. They're really green and I don't know anyone with green eyes and I think I kind of got lost, in your eyes." I couldn't believe those words had actually just left my mouth. What an idiot I was. I just told a girl that I just met that I got lost in her eyes. I mean who does something stupid like that?

"Mike," Liz sat up in her seat, hands folded on her desk, her cheeks turning pink. "That was such a sweet thing to say." Her face glowed as she looked at me, and then turned away, embarrassed.

What? She thought I was sweet? I thought I was an idiot. She thought I was sweet!

She let out an audible sigh and turned back to me. "So if you're done gazing into my beautiful eyes," she laughed and batted her eye lashes, "maybe we can get back to the project now."

I had to do a quick reality check. I just met a

very cute girl. This girl was smart, funny and, did I

mention, cute?   And, we were going to be working

together on a project.   I also learned that when I think

I'm being an idiot, I'm actually quite sweet. None of

this made any sense to me, but then again, there

wasn't a lot that was making sense lately.

Chapter 30

Liz and I spent the next thirty minutes talking about everything except the project. I found out that we like mostly the same music and movies. And, as it turns out, she did play in the band, clarinet. She had tried gymnastics but had broken a bone in her foot and hand during a competition. Her doctor said she had to stop because of growth plates or something like that. She loved horses and went riding with friends of hers from another school. She had been on high honor roll ever since she started school. And, she had always thought I was cute.

It was amazing. I was even more amazed and really disappointed, when Mrs. Perkins announced that it was time to wrap up and that class was over. Thirty minutes seemed like three minutes.

"We didn't even talk about the project," Liz said as she stood. She reached into her book bag, pulled out a blue folder and handed it to me. "Last weekend I started looking up some of the stuff we'll need just to get a head start. I made some copies of things and put them together for you. Look them over if you get the chance."

I took the folder from her, not wanting our conversation or our time together to end. "Listen, I know we just met and everything, but do you want to get together after school to go over some of this?"

Liz thought for a second. She had a way of looking off into the distance to gather her thoughts. She turned back to me with a smile. "Sure. Let's meet in the library after school."   She smiled at me sweetly and left the room.

I gathered my things, and, lost in thought, I walked toward the door.

"How did it go, Michael? Did you two hit it off okay?" It was Mrs. Perkins.

"Oh, not too bad," I stammered. "I think this will be a lot of fun."

Chapter 31

My last class of the day was gym and it was the only class I shared with Rosie. The gym teacher, who was also the basketball coach, spent ten minutes trying to recruit us all for the basketball team. It was still September and basketball didn't start until November, but that didn't matter. For the first ten minutes of every gym class, we'd get a sales pitch from the coach about playing hoops. Once he was done, he threw out some basketballs, and surprise, surprise, told us to go and shoot.

Rosie and I found a basket at the far end of the gym and began shooting the ball. I told him all about social studies and Liz Lorman and meeting her after school.

"Mikey, Liz is a cutie." Rosie said, as he rebounded my missed shot. "We were in fourth grade together. She's pretty smart, too."

"Cool," I said as I took another shot. "She is kind of short though, like an elf," I added.

Rosie tried to grab another of my missed rebounds. The ball bounced off his hands and rolled toward the back wall as he chased it. He returned with the ball, slightly out of breath, but instead of throwing it back, he walked over and held it out to me. As I reached for it, he held on tightly until I looked him in the face.

"Listen," Rosie said, still catching his breath. "I'm kind of chunky. She's kind of short. I don't like it when people talk about other people like that. I know it happens and I expect it to happen, but not from my best friends." Rosie had made his point but he wasn't done yet. "The truth of it is that no one is perfect, we all have our issues, and it's just that some of them are easier to see."

"Sorry, Rosie," I knew he could be sensitive about his weight and about saying things about other people. He and I would joke about it sometimes, but other times, like now, he reminded me that some jokes aren't funny. And he was right about everyone having their own issues. I sure had mine.

I pulled on the ball, but Rosie still didn't let go. "Can I have the ball now?" I asked.

Rosie pulled it back hard, "No way, man. You missed two shots in a row." He laughed as he dribbled away, then he turned back. "Besides, I got a question for you and, if I make the shot, I'll ask you, and if I miss it, I won't."

"Whatever," I said, trying to be cool and pretending not to care. "I don't care."

"Oh, you might care about this one," he laughed. Rosie dribbled the ball a couple more times and it rolled off his foot. He may have had a way with the girls, but he was not an athlete. He chased it down near the basket, turned without looking and sank the shot. Maybe I spoke too soon. Rosie threw his hands up in the air and did a little dance that made me laugh.

"So?" I asked. "What is it?'

Rosie walked over and placed his hand on my shoulder. "It's really a pretty simple question," he said, as he turned me to face the other side of the gym,

where Melissa Burns stood, waiting for me to walk her

home. "What are you going to do about *that*?

Chapter 32

The gym teacher blew his whistle, and after we picked up all of the basketballs, we were dismissed for the day. I walked over to the doors where Melissa was waiting.

"Hey," she said, as she flipped her long blond hair back away from her face.

"Hey." I replied, carrying my backpack instead of slinging it over my shoulder. It seemed like the cool thing to do. She still smelled wonderful.

"Are you ready to go?" she asked.

I hesitated. First of all, Craig had recently threatened to kill me if I talked to Melissa again. The stench of his breath was gone but the left side of my chest was still sore from the finger poke. If I was smart, I'd have run from the gym screaming, but the sight of Melissa somehow overrode my brain's instinct to run away. I know that there is some kind of biological term for what was happening in my head, but I had no idea what it was.

But I also hesitated for a second reason. I knew that Liz was sitting in the library waiting for me. I wondered how this sort of thing happens to a kid like me. How do I go from a geek without a single girl in the school even knowing I was alive, to a geek with two girls who both seem to like me? The problem here is that I've never ever had this problem before. I mean, I've hardly even talked to a girl this much. And now I've got two of them who want to talk to me and I have to decide which one to talk to. Melissa and Liz were both great but they were both so different. That left me with a huge decision and no easy answer.

"I forgot that I was supposed to meet a friend in the library to work on a project." I said, still unsure of what I wanted to do.

Melissa instantly looked disappointed. "Oh, I was hoping we could walk together and talk."

"Ok," I replied with a smile. I was so confused. Of course I knew Liz was waiting in the library, but Melissa was right here, waiting for me to walk her home. Is this what all of the cool kids go through?

Melissa and I walked down the hall and out the side doors into the warm and sunny afternoon. We started talking about things we liked and didn't like, and that led to a discussion of our favorite teachers and classes. Melissa began telling me about her algebra test and I listened as much as I could. It was hard to concentrate because, well, I was walking Melissa Burns home and every kid in school was watching us walk out together. I could imagine the whispers. 'There's the hot girl and that zombie kid walking home together.'

A cool breeze greeted us as we rounded the corner of the building heading down the sidewalk. Melissa paused to shiver and then continued to talk. Her words faded into the background as a chill ran through me. But wait a minute, the ghost had already appeared earlier today. It had never shown up twice in one day, it had always needed time to rest. And I had never seen it outside. Despite this logic, the sensation was unmistakable even if it didn't make sense. I tried to convince myself that he couldn't appear now. Not in the daylight, in the middle of the afternoon. Not after having appeared already today. My heart began to race as I tried to figure out what was going on.

Melissa's cell phone rang with a song and she stopped and looked at the screen. "It's my dad, I have to take this." I watched as she put a finger in her left ear and placed the phone up to her right ear. She turned and walked off the sidewalk and away from me to talk.

As I looked back in the direction we were going, there was the ghost standing about ten feet in front of me. I moved backward, my backpack falling from my shoulder. His face was curled into a snarl as he pointed at me. His body took shape and form and, unlike anything you see in the movies, I was unable to see through him. He looked like he was a real person standing before me, and that made him seem all the more frightening. He pointed at me again, only this time with more ferocity. Then I realized, he wasn't pointing at me, he was pointing at my backpack.

"All set?" Melissa asked.

I looked at her, and then looked back to the sidewalk. The ghost was gone.

Chapter 33

I walked Melissa to her house and we talked on the porch for a minute before she said goodbye and went inside. It didn't even cross my mind to wonder about a kiss. How crazy is that? I just walked the best looking girl in the school home and I wasn't even thinking about a kiss. It could have been my first kiss with a girl who wasn't my mom and I blew it. I mean you would think kissing Melissa Burns would have been the only thing on my mind. Instead, the image on the sidewalk continued to haunt me, and for many reasons. First, this was definitely an angry ghost with a bad temper. He hadn't done any harm to me yet, but each new sighting seemed to bring about a new level of rage. Secondly, the ghost had materialized twice in the same day. Thirdly, he materialized in broad

185

daylight and in a full form that made him look real.

Once I got home, I sat at the kitchen table, my backpack before me. He was clearly pointing at the bag, which must mean that there is something in there he wanted. I took a deep breath and unzipped the pack. I pulled out all of the folders and loose papers that cluttered most of it. It was only my first day back, so there really wasn't the usual amount of garbage that seemed to always fill my backpack. I pulled out some pens and pencils.   There was a half-broken chocolate Pop-Tart in a baggie and some empty gum wrappers. And that was it.

I sat back wondering what I was supposed to be looking for. The only new papers I had today were a study packet from science, a math homework sheet, and the folder that Liz had given me. I pulled the blue folder from the pile and opened it. Inside was the information sheet on our project. Under that was an index card with 'MASON WAREHOUSE' written neatly in red letters. That must have been the card that Liz had picked. In the opposite pocket of the folder I found copies from internet searches about the warehouse. I flipped through the papers until one headline caught my eye.

Warehouse Fire Suspect Found Guilty

Now Faces Death Penalty

I quickly scanned the article, then turned the page. Instantly my skin tingled with goose bumps. I felt my mouth drop open as I stared at a color picture of my ghost. The words 'Found Guilty' were written

above the photo and the name 'Travis Cleveland Riley'
was written underneath.

There he was. My throat went dry and my
palms became sweaty as I stared at the picture. My
ghost, the article claimed, had set fire to the Mason
Warehouse, killing a warehouse manager and another
employee. I scanned the next article, my heart racing
as it told of how the jury had taken only minutes to
find the defendant guilty of arson and murder. The
article went on to say that the judge in the case
scolded the defendant and then sentenced him to
death.

The more I read, the more frightened I became.
Now the ghost had a name, and somehow that seemed
to make him more terrifying. Even worse, the ghost

that had followed me back from the dead was an

arsonist and a murderer.

Chapter 34

I called Mrs. Grey and she was at my house in fifteen minutes. I told her everything that had happened and showed her the articles and the picture.

"See," I pointed to the article, "He's a murderer. He killed people and he followed me back here. I think we need to get some help. A priest, a witch doctor, a voodoo dude- whatever we need, but I want him gone."

Mrs. Grey hummed as she often did. She picked up the page with the photo and gazed at it again. "I'm not usually one for judging a book by its cover, Michael, but now that I can see what you've been seeing, I understand why you've been so frightened. He's a very devilish- looking fellow."

"Yeah," I muttered, "you should see him in person. Trust me, it's much worse!"

Mrs. Grey sat back and folded her hands. "My grandmother told me an interesting story sometime ago. It seems that, when she was first married, there was a man living next door to her, Mr. Goodman I think his name was. She described Mr. Goodman as the most handsome man she had ever seen; even more handsome than her own husband, although she would never tell him that, of course. She described him as angelic, like a Greek god. Mr. Goodman was also very well liked by everyone in the community. He was successful and handsome, quite a catch, I was told."

"Is this going somewhere?" I interrupted.

Mrs. Grey gave me a stern look, and then

continued, "It seems that Mr. Goodman had a fondness for imported ice cream. I can't imagine how much that must have cost him." Mrs. Grey mused. "One day the gentleman who delivered the ice cream arrived at Mr. Goodman's house to find him gone. Not wanting to leave the ice cream outside and knowing that he would not make this delivery round for another two weeks, he opened the garage door and let himself into the garage where Mr. Goodman kept a large freezer that always stored his ice cream. Upon opening the freezer door, the delivery man found it full, full of frozen corpses, that is. Needless to say, after the police found him, Mr. Goodman did not get to enjoy any of his imported ice cream."

I looked at Mrs. Grey, dumbfounded. I didn't understand what this had to do with anything. "Mrs.

Grey, I don't understand what this has to do with anything."

Mrs. Grey smiled, "You see Michael, Mr. Goodman, the man with the angelic face, turned out to be a devil. Perhaps your ghost, your man with the devil's face will turn out differently than you think."

This was becoming a pattern now. I would complain to Mrs. Grey. She would somehow twist all of the words around until they made sense when they weren't supposed to and it would always end up with me having to talk to the scariest ghost I've ever seen. Yes, I know this is the only ghost I've ever seen. And to top it off, I just found out that this one's a killer. Great!

I took a deep breath, trying to calm myself

before responding to Mrs. Grey. "The paper said he murdered two people. He had a trial, they found him guilty and they fried him. He obviously spent some time just hanging around until I died, and now he spends his free time popping in and out of my life and making scary faces at me. I think you might be off on this one Mrs. Grey."

"Could be, Michael," she began. "However, he did ask for your help. He did try to get you to leave the bathroom before the bullies came in. He did point to the backpack that contained the folder that told you who he was. It seems like he's gone through an awful lot of trouble to get your attention. If he was so terrible, if he meant you harm, why go to all of the trouble? Hmmm... I think *you* might be off on this one, Michael."

I sat back in thought. I liked Mrs. Grey a lot better when I had hated her.

Chapter 35

I walked into social studies class the next day and noticed that Liz was not in her seat. I scanned the room, but no Liz.

"What are you doing here, Michael?" asked Mrs. Perkins.

"I, uh, was coming to class?" I replied, unsure of the correct answer.

"Liz is in the library. She asked me last bell if your group could just go there to work today. I would have thought you knew about it. Didn't you two talk about your plans for the project?"

"Oh, yeah, we did. I must have forgotten."

"You know, I find the most successful groups

are the ones that communicate well and cooperate

together. I hope you two are doing that." She

cautioned with that tone that all teachers have.

I excused myself and headed down the hall

toward the library. This was going to be

uncomfortable.

As I walked in, I found Liz sitting in the back by

herself, papers scattered across the table. I stood

before her as she worked and I waited for her to look

up. She didn't.

"So you finally decided to show up?" she asked,

still working away. Usually people can tell if someone is

angry or disappointed by the sound of their voice, but I

couldn't sense either of those from Liz.

I pulled out the chair across from her and sat

down. She continued to work. "Liz listen, I'm really sorry about yesterday."

"That's fine," she replied in an even voice.

"No, it's not fine. I'm really sorry."

Liz put her pencil down and finally looked up at me. In a calm voice she began, "I know I'm not tall and blonde and beautiful. You did what most boys would do. How can I be mad about that?" Liz picked her pencil back up. "I just thought you weren't like most boys. It was my mistake." Liz added as she went back to work.

I scrambled to try and think of the right words to say. There was only one thought that came to mind. "I know I messed up yesterday. Maybe I can make it up to you by telling you something, something about me that no one knows. And I mean no one, not my mom, not Rosie or Tom. "

Liz looked up, obviously intrigued by what I had offered. She put her pencil down again. "Go on."

Even though there was no one else around, I leaned in close across the table, to be sure that no one did hear what I was about to say. "You know how I died?

Liz nodded.

"Well," I continued, "when I came back, something came back with me. I'm being haunted by a ghost."

Liz looked at me. She smiled sweetly, "I was really wrong about you. You're not like other guys."

Liz leaned back and her voice escalated as she

continued, "You're worse! You're a JERK!"

Chapter 36

Liz stood up and began packing up her papers in a huff. "You can find another partner and do your own project! Or you can just take this one and I'll get another project to do."

I stood up half-expecting the librarian to show up. "Liz, I'm not lying to you," I began. "I know you don't owe me any favors, but just listen to what I have to say. If you don't believe me when I'm done, I'll give you back all of the information and tell Mrs. Perkins that I want to work by myself and I promise I won't bother you again."

Liz paused in her frantic stacking of papers and glared at me. "You want to tell me your story?" she began. "Fine, I'll be here after school. If you want to talk, be here five minutes after the last bell. If you're just one minute late, I don't ever want to see you again." She finished collecting her papers and left me standing at the table.

"Young man," I heard a man behind me say. "We have rules in the library. My library." I turned to find the librarian, Mrs. Gilmore. She was tough, mean and had a crew cut and, oh yeah, she had a man's voice. Not just any man's voice, but like a drill sergeant's voice. "And if you plan on spending any more time here during the next several years of your education, you will refrain from loud and vulgar language. Are we clear?"

"Yes ma'am." I replied in an almost whisper.

"I said are we clear?" She repeated loudly.

"Yes," I replied loudly enough for her to hear.

She scowled and marched off to terrorize some other poor kid I'm sure.

I turned and headed out the door to my remaining classes, deep in thought. Other than Mrs. Grey, Liz would be the only person to know my secret. I'm not sure why I felt the need to tell her. It just seemed like she was someone I could trust. And it had to be more than just coincidence that she and I shared a project that involved my ghost.

Chapter 37

After the last bell, I began to quickly make my way across the school, back to the library. I did not want to be late. As I walked down the last part of the hall, with the library doors in sight, two large hands grabbed me under each arm and forcefully turned me toward the boy's bathroom, using my chest as the door opener. As I was shoved into the bathroom, there stood Craig. His two big goons pushed me onto the floor at his feet.

Oddly enough, my first thought was, 'what is it with bathrooms? It seems like every time I'm near one there's a bully or a ghost waiting for me.'

"I guess you didn't pay attention during our little talk yesterday," Craig said, as he moved forward and stepped heavily on the fingers of my right hand. "If you start screaming, then I'll have to shut you up, so don't even think about it," he snarled, as he twisted his foot for what seemed like an hour, and then finally released my hand. My fingers throbbed in pain.

"Let me kick him, Craig," one of the goons said. His work boot-covered foot was enormous. He could have kicked me across the room with it.

"Stand him up," Craig ordered and the two goons grabbed me under the arms again and brought me to my feet. Craig stepped up until his face was inches from mine. "I told you to stay away from Melissa. When I say stay away, do you know what that means?"

His breath still smelled like a dog's which made

my eyes involuntarily water and want to close. I couldn't help it but my face scrunched into an expression like I had just bitten into a lemon. How can someone with such white teeth have such smelly breath? Maybe it was because I was overwhelmed by the shine of Craig's teeth and the dog breath, that I didn't feel the temperature change.

"Dude, did it just get freez'n in here?" asked the smaller of the two giant goons.

"Whoa, yeah," replied the other, as I saw his breath like a mist coming over my shoulder.

Suddenly, the first sink in the row of five sinks began to stream water from the faucet. One by one the others all turned on by themselves, spewing water with force into the basins. I felt the grip of the goons loosen as they watched the sink water roaring full blast, all on their own. Craig looked to the sinks, then back to me again, uncertainty in his eyes. He was more curious than scared, ...at least so far.

"WHAM," the door to the farthest bathroom stall slammed shut, echoing like thunder, then opened itself and slammed again. "WHAM!" Now the second of the stall doors joined in opening and slamming all by itself. The lights began to flicker, creating a strobe-like effect. The goons released me, stepped back and fled the bathroom. Craig's head was turned toward the slamming doors but as he looked back for his friends, I saw in the flickering light between the darkness, that he was terrified. He stepped back away from the doors, then turned and sprinted from the bathroom.

Slowly the water began to subside to a slow drip. The doors swung gently to a stop, the lights stayed steady and the temperature returned to normal. My ghost had saved me!

"Thank you," I said, my voice echoing quietly in the empty bathroom.

Chapter 38

"Liz!"

I ran from the bathroom and down the hall to the library. I threw open the door and immediately caught the gaze of Mrs. Gilmore. She scowled, pointed two fingers to her eyes then pointed to mine, letting me know that she was watching me. My pace slowed from a run to a quick walk as I made my way to the back table, her glare following me as I went. I rounded the corner to find the table empty and a feeling of great disappointment. I was late and Liz had left. I set my bag under the table and sat down, wondering what to do next.

"So what's all of this talk about a ghost?" I heard Liz say from behind me.

"You *are* here!" I said pointing out the obvious.

Liz walked to the other side of the table,

dropped her book bag and sat down. "So," she began,

"you were kind of a jerk for just leaving me here

yesterday. And I'm saying that as your partner. It's

not like we're dating or anything." There was a brief

pause, almost an awkward silence. Then she smiled

and spoke again, "You apologized and now I want to

hear about this ghost."

Liz smiled and I knew that things with us were

back to okay again. "Have you ever seen a ghost?" I

asked.

"No. My cousin swears that she's seen a ghost

in the house she used to live in and she told me all

about it, but I've never seen one. I love watching all of

those ghost shows on TV. So I guess I kind of believe."

"Well, I'd never seen one either. And honestly I don't even know if I thought they were real, but I do now. Liz, everything I'm about to tell you is the absolute truth," and so I explained everything from the time that I jumped into the pool, right up to the bathroom event just minutes ago. Liz listened intently and from her expressions I could tell she believed what I was telling her.

When I was done I said, "There's one more thing. And this is the really creepy part." I pulled the blue folder she had given me from my backpack and removed the picture of Travis Cleveland Riley and slid it across the table.

Liz's face went white and I could actually see

211

goosebumps rise on her arms as she put the information together in her head. "No Way," she whispered.

"Yes," I said. "Travis Cleveland Riley followed me back from the dead. It's taken a while to figure out, but I'm pretty sure he wants my help. I have no idea where to start, Liz. I didn't even know who he was until you handed me this folder. So, if I'm going to help him, I'm going to need you to help me."

Color returned to Liz's face and her goosebumps faded. "Let's get started," she said.

Chapter 39

Liz suggested that we reread all of the information that she had collected so far and take notes on anything that might be useful. Next, we'd get back on the internet and do some more research. The hard part about this big mystery was we still didn't know what the ghost wanted. Liz thought that maybe the more we knew about the background of the warehouse and Travis Cleveland Riley, the easier it might be to figure it all out.

I found an online encyclopedia that gave a summary of the Mason Warehouse and Liz asked me read it aloud.

"The Mason Warehouse was built in the early nineteen hundreds by Gordon Mason. At the time, there were a large number of successful factories in

the city. The factories needed a place to store

materials that they would use to make their products

and to store the finished products when they were

done. During World War I and II, the government

leased part of the warehouse to store standard military

equipment like uniforms and general supplies. The

warehouse became one of the more successful

businesses in town."

"This all seems kind of boring to me," I said.

"Keep reading," Liz replied.

"In 1974, founder and owner Gordon Mason

died at the age of 86. His company was left in the

hands of his daughter, Linda Mason. In the late 1970's

urban renewal swept through much of the city and

many of the factories that had been staples of the

community began to close. The warehouse weathered

the economic downfall only to face more serious

problems in the late 1980's when, due to advancement

in computer technology, many of the remaining

factories were forced to close. By 1995 the Mason

warehouse was in debt in the amount of nearly two

and a half million dollars."

"Wow," Liz interrupted, "they owed a lot of

money."

"In March of 1998, a fire destroyed the

warehouse, killing the warehouse manager and the

business accountant. Despite a lack of eyewitness

evidence, Travis Cleveland Riley was convicted of

setting the fire and of murder, and was executed on

August 17th of the following year. The amount of the insurance settlement was never disclosed but was believed to be in the seven million dollar range. Linda Mason sold the destroyed warehouse and property back to the city which turned the property into a parking garage."

Liz grabbed my hand. "Go back," she yelled.

"Back to what?" I asked in surprise.

"When did they execute Travis?"

"It says August 17th of the following year..." My voice trailed off as I suddenly realized the importance of the date. "August 17th was the day of my accident."

"That means you and Travis died on the same day, twelve years apart."

Chapter 40

"We need to find out more about the ghost…, I mean Travis," Liz said. "There's got to be more information out there on him."

Liz searched the computer again and found a number of newspaper articles related to the fire and the trial. Finally, in a Sunday edition of the city paper, she found an interview with Travis's mom that was written a week after Travis had been convicted. There was a picture of Travis's mom in a wheelchair. She looked old and poor and worn down by life. Liz scanned the article then said, "Listen to this, it's his mom talking about Travis."

"Travis was always kind of hard on his luck. He was born with a birth defect that made him kind of slow in school. He tried, but much of that school stuff was way above his head. Travis was such a simple boy and school didn't have a place for him. 'Cause he was so slow, and maybe 'cause we didn't have much money for fine clothes and such, kids used to pick on him something awful.   By the time he was eleven or so, he been beaten up more times than I care to remember.   It was just me and him and he didn't have no daddy to look to. About then he went and made his mind up to not getting beaten anymore and whenever there was an issue after that, Travis would finish it good. Most kids stopped picking on him then, but there was some that always wanted to fight him. Travis started getting in some trouble about then, in his teenage years. It was mostly just defending himself against bullies, but cops don't care who started the fight. That's why he'd been arrested a couple of times. But I will tell you something about Travis; he is a boy inside a man's body. I'm sure that he has no idea why he's been arrested and sentenced to die. I asked him if he set that fire and he told me no. My boy has never, and I mean never, lied to me. Travis didn't set that fire anymore than you or I did. He's a good boy."

Liz skimmed ahead in the article and said, "Okay listen to this part: The reporter asked his mom, 'if Travis was such a good kid, why was everyone afraid of him.'

"I think there is two reasons for that. Like I told you, Travis got to a point where if he was afraid to get beat up, he would go ahead and throw the first punch when kids started picking on him. Once he got started, it was like he lost his mind and there were plenty of kids who got a good whooping from Travis. The second reason..."

Liz read ahead quietly then stopped to tell me that the reporter noted that, for the first time in the interview with Travis's mom, she began to cry.

"The second reason everyone was afraid of Travis is that he never smiled. The last picture I have of him smiling is when he was eight years old. After that he was getting teased and picked on and beaten all the time. He was such a happy baby, used to smile all the time. But after what he had to live through, no father, me in a wheelchair, dirt poor and getting teased all the time, I don't blame him for never smiling again."

We both sat in silence for a minute. In the past hour I had felt two very new and different emotions for Travis other than fear and terror. I had felt grateful when he saved me from getting beaten up by Craig. And now I felt sorry for him for having to grow up the way he did.

Chapter 41

Liz spoke first, her voice full of emotion, "How sad."

"I know," I replied.

"What are you thinking?" she asked

I hesitated before answering because even I couldn't believe what I was about to say. "I think Travis wants us to prove that he didn't start the fire."

"I think you're right," Liz added with determination.

"I think we're crazy." I said, sliding my chair back from the computer screen. "I mean really, we're just kids. How are we supposed to prove someone innocent of a crime that happened twelve years ago?

It's impossible. If Travis really wanted someone to solve his crime couldn't he have haunted a lawyer or a cop or something?"

"Just how many lawyers and cops do you think die and come back to life every day?" she asked sarcastically. "Think about it for a minute. People were afraid of Travis. If you had to frame someone for a crime, why not someone who was scary and tough and simple-minded? The article said Travis and his mom were poor, so there was no way they could afford a good lawyer."

"That's a pretty thin theory," I replied trying to sound like an attorney I had seen on TV.

"Yeah," Liz came back, "well, how about owing millions of dollars and suddenly your warehouse burns down and you collect twice as much as you owed?"

"That's a better sounding theory," I had to admit, even though I didn't want to.

Liz's green eyes sparkled as she made her point, "Put them both together and it makes a really great theory."

"So where do we start?" I asked reluctantly.

"We already have," Liz replied with a smile.

Chapter 42

It was getting late and the library would be closing soon, so Liz and I agreed to stop for the day. She called her mom for a ride and I walked home. Even after the near disaster with her just a day ago, we had a pretty good afternoon.

I had just gotten in my house when the doorbell rang. It was Rosie and Tom. I grabbed some popsicles and we went outside.

"Why do you always give me the orange popsicle?" Tom asked, as he took a bite.

"Because nobody likes the orange ones," I replied.

"I don't like the orange ones," he responded.

"Yeah, but you eat them. That's why I give them to you."

Tom shook his head in disgust and took another bite.

"I sure do love the purple ones," Rosie had to add, as he licked his purple popsicle.

I decided to change the subject before we got into an all out popsicle argument. Before I could think of something to say, Rosie changed the subject for me.

"So, I heard that Craig wants to beat you up. What's up with that?"

"I don't know," I replied. "He and his goons dragged me into the bathroom today. I was lucky to get away."

"I know why he's trying to give you a beat down," Tom began, "because you've been all mushy-mushy with Melissa."

"Mushy-mushy?" I asked.

"Yeah, you know, making out with her," Tom said.

I laughed. "I have not been making out with her. We're just friends right now."

"I'd be making out with her if I were you," Tom said with certainty.

Rosie looked at Tom and began to laugh, "Who have you ever made out with?"

"Plenty of girls," Tom replied, defensively.

"Oh sure, I forgot, there's your mom, your

grandma, your aunt, your sister, the old lady at the

lunch counter," Rosie laughed harder.

"Whatever," Tom returning back to his

popsicle. "Listen," he said looking at me and sounding

serious, "you just need to watch your back because if

Craig gets the chance, he'll pound you."

I knew Tom was right. I had help from Travis

last time, but I couldn't count on that to happen again.

If Craig got to me without my friends or without Travis,

I was a dead man.

Chapter 43

After the guys left, I made myself some dinner, a hot dog and some potato chips and watched some TV. For the first time in weeks, I walked around the house unafraid. Partially because Travis had appeared three times in the last two days so I didn't expect to see him again soon, but mostly because now I thought I knew why Travis needed my help.

I began to wonder how Liz and I could ever prove that Travis was innocent. This wasn't a cop show where everything is solved in an hour. This was real life. And in this real life, two sixth-graders were trying to solve a twelve-year-old crime. The more I thought about it, the more it made my head hurt and made me depressed. I decided to call Mrs. Grey.

I told her about the recent attack by Craig and his thugs and how Travis had saved me. I also told her about the information that Liz and I had uncovered so far. Mrs. Grey had remembered the warehouse fire being a big news story at the time, but couldn't remember any of the details.

"I don't know what to do," I told her. "I think Travis wants us to prove that he didn't start the fire and kill those people and I want to try to help. Liz and I can look all we want at old pictures and papers, but we can't go back to see what happened. We don't have any way to prove that he didn't do it."

Mrs. Grey was silent for a moment. "I wish I had some advice for you, Michael," she began. "The only thing I can offer is what I do when I have a very difficult problem and don't know how to solve it."

"What is it?" I asked excitedly.

"I go to sleep," she replied.

"What?"

"I go to sleep. When I wake up in the morning, the answer is right there in my head. It's like it had been there all along, but I just couldn't reach it."

"You go to sleep," I said again, unconvinced.

"Give it a try, dear. You've had a very busy few days and I'm sure you must be exhausted. You might be amazed at what a good night's sleep will do for you."

Mrs. Grey and I finished our conversation and I still had no answer as to how to help Travis. Maybe she was right, I began to wonder. I did feel a little tired. Maybe I needed to clear my head.

Mom got home from work around eight. She was happy because I had picked up the kitchen, something I did more often now, since Mrs. Grey. We had some popcorn and sat and talked for a while. Later, we played a game and sure enough, I was tired. We said good night and I went to bed. I slept like a rock. When the alarm rang in the morning, I hit the snooze and waited to see if an answer had magically appeared overnight. By the time the second alarm went off, I realized that I still had no answer.

Chapter 44

The next few days were spent avoiding Craig and continuing to work on the information we had found about Travis. Neither were that easy to do. I tried to be cautious when I walked down the hallway now, and always tried to look ahead to see if I could see Craig and his goons. Once or twice I would have to duck into a classroom and wait for them to pass before I went on my way. But so far, the last few days were virtually Craig-free.

The information we uncovered on Travis and the fire was basically more of what we already knew. We read countless articles and interviews with the police and workers from the Mason Warehouse. Yet even with all of our hard work, there was nothing that stood out that would help us help Travis.

On Friday, I had agreed to meet Liz in the library after school. This time *she* was late. I was reading through our notes when a book crashed into the back of my head with a loud 'thwap!' I looked down and it was *Tom Sawyer*, that book by Mark Twain. It was a pretty big book. I turned around and there was Craig. Before I could move he was behind me, his hands digging into my shoulders as I sat. He leaned down close to me.

"Haven't seen you in a few days Zombie," he began. "I know you've been hiding, but you'll need to find a bigger school if you want to hide from me." He squeezed his hands deeper into my neck and shoulders.

"Ow!"

Craig relaxed his grip slightly. "I don't know what happened in the bathroom this week, but whatever freak-show it was, it isn't going to stop me from kicking your butt."

"Craig," came a man's voice. It was Mrs. Gilmore. "Craig, are you okay?"

She was asking if *he* was okay? He's squeezing my shoulders like a stress ball and she wants to know if he's alright?

"I'm fine, Mrs. Gilmore. I was just having a chat with Michael here. He dropped his book on the floor and I told him he should pick it up. You don't treat books, let alone classics like *Tom Sawyer*, that way." Craig smiled, his hands now resting on my shoulders.

Mrs. Gilmore's eyes narrowed and her gaze fell upon me. "Pick up *Tom Sawyer* this instant," she barked. "You need to have more respect for this library, young man. Back in the day, I would have taken a ruler to your knuckles by now, you snot-nosed little punk."

I picked up the book and set it next to me on the table. Did she just call me a snot-nosed little punk? Can she do that?

"Thank you, Craig. We need more fine young men like you around this building."

"Oh, you're welcome, Mrs. Gilmore," Craig squeezed my shoulders one last time, then slapped me hard on the back and looked at me. "You treat those books with respect, and don't you dare give Mrs.

Gilmore a hard time."

Craig walked past the warmest smile Mrs. Gilmore was capable of and out of the library. Mrs. Gilmore actually growled at me, then walked away.

Not wanting to face her wrath again, I mumbled the random thoughts racing through my head under my breath instead of yelling them out loud. "I hope Craig didn't hurt his hands squeezing the life out of me. *Tom Sawyer* is a stupid book. It's heavy and it hurts when it hits you in the head. I hate this library. I wish you would go back to the Marines and fight with people your own age."

Chapter 45

I felt better after mumbling all of that. I could have done more but that seemed to make my point. I picked up the notes from where I had left off before *Tom Sawyer* bonked me in the head, when Liz came bopping around the corner. Her red curls bounced as she plunked herself down in the seat next to me, grabbed my arm and smiled.

"I've got great news," she said excitedly. Her enthusiasm was contagious and her hands felt warm on the skin of my arm. It made me forget all about Craig and Mrs. Gilmore. "I did some more research and guess what I found?"

"Ah?" was all that came out because I didn't have a guess.

Her face lit up as she said, "I found out that Linda Mason is still alive!" She waited a few seconds for my response but could tell I wasn't totally impressed yet, so she continued. "And, guess what? We have an interview with her tomorrow afternoon!"

"What? How did you get an interview with her?" I asked.

"I just called. I told her we were doing a class project on the Mason Warehouse and she agreed to talk with us. It was that simple."

"Oh, and are we just going to ask her, 'By the way, do you know who really set fire to the warehouse?'" I asked.

Some of the excitement faded from Liz's green eyes. "No, but we'll get the chance to talk to her.

Maybe we can find more information."

"Yeah, maybe we can ask her what she did with the millions of dollars she got after the insurance settlement." I said. I know I was being kind of a jerk, but I didn't really want to go and talk to some old lady I didn't know about a crime that happened twelve years ago.

Liz took her hands off my arm. "Are you reading *Tom Sawyer*?" she asked quietly.

"No," I said with a snarky reply. And before I could explain what had happened earlier, she picked up the book and cracked me in the head with it, making another loud thwap. I had never even seen a copy of *Tom Sawyer* until today, and twice now I've been hit in the head with it. I'm pretty sure I hate that book.

"Listen," Liz insisted, sounding both of impatient and spunky, "we've got a great opportunity here. I'll do the talking if you're nervous. The whole reason this started is because Travis needs our help and maybe by talking to Linda Mason, we can get some answers."

I knew Liz was right, but that didn't mean I had to like it. Finally, I sighed. "Okay, we'll do it. Just don't hit me with that book again."

Liz jumped up from her seat and hugged me. "Yes!" she said. "Trust me. This will all work out."

The hug startled me, but I hugged her back. She sat back in her seat and her expression changed as she looked over my shoulder.

241

"Hi Mikey," came the familiar voice of Melissa Burns.

Chapter 46

I could feel my face turn red as I gazed up at the ever-gorgeous Melissa Burns. Her blond hair hung loosely over her shoulders and I could tell she had just put something on her lips because they glistened like they were dipped in a pool of sparkling wax. "Hey, Melissa," was all I could manage to say.

"I haven't seen you in a few days and Rosie said he thought you might still be in the library studying." Melissa flipped her hair over her shoulder and briefly looked at Liz, then back to me. "I was wondering if you wanted to walk home together?"

There was an awkward moment of silence, mostly because I didn't know what to say. I looked at Liz and then at Melissa. After what seemed like forever, Liz slid her chair back, stood up and began gathering her things. "We were just about done, anyways." Liz said as she picked up her backpack. She smiled at me then looked up at Melissa, who was noticeably taller. She looked back at me and said, "I'll text you tomorrow morning about our meeting. Have a good walk home." She flung her pack over her shoulder, and with that she was gone.

"She is so cute," Melissa began. "It's so nice of you to work on a project with her." I couldn't tell from her expression or the sound of her voice if she was being sincere or sarcastic. I would have said something but I didn't know what to say.

I gathered my things and Melissa and I walked out of the library. We left the school through the side doors that always creaked and began our walk down the bumpy, cracked sidewalk in the warm afternoon sun. We finally started to talk a little bit about the week, and then went back to walking quietly. Before I knew it, we were at the familiar place where Travis had appeared the last time we were on our way home. It had been several days since I had seen him, so I was feeling a little uneasy about what might lie ahead this time.

Melissa must have sensed that I was lost in thought and she bumped into me, in a flirty way, which got my attention. I bumped her back. "So there was something I wanted to ask you," she began. "There's a dance coming up next Friday, and I don't have anyone to go with. It's the first dance of the year so it should be a lot of fun. Anyways, I was wondering if you'd want to take me?"

Now, most guys would have yelled 'YES' right away. I mean, Melissa Burns just asked me, *yes me*, a previously unknown dork, to the dance. But for some reason, the word 'yes' did not come out of my mouth. "Next Friday, huh? Well I'll have to check with my mom and make sure that there isn't anything going on."

Melissa stopped walking and turned to face me. "It would really mean a lot to me if you went," she said, her lips glistening even more in the sunlight.

I was in a trance. I heard the words, "um, okay?" come tumbling out of my mouth.

In a flash, Melissa smiled, then leaned in and gave me a kiss on the cheek. "I'll call you tomorrow," she beamed. And with that, she turned the corner and was on her way home. I stood in shocked silence trying to understand what had just happened. The hottest girl in the school just asked me to a dance and then she kissed me. Wow! This was everything I wanted. Yet, somehow, I didn't feel as happy as I think I should have.

Chapter 47

After a couple of back and forth texts with Liz
on Saturday morning, I told her that my mom would
drive us to our meeting with Linda Mason. Liz lived in
an apartment complex a few miles away. Not that my
neighborhood is the greatest or anything, but as we
drove closer to Liz's place, I could see a change in the
houses and the people. Many of the houses were in
obvious need of a paint job or repair and some needed
the lawn mowed. There were a lot of people who
were dressed in old or dirty clothes. They sat on their
porches or seemed to wander about without purpose.
It wasn't the worst section of town, but it was right
next door to it. Let's just say I wouldn't want to be lost
there in the dark.

When we arrived, Liz was sitting outside the apartment waiting for us as we pulled up. She stood up and, with a notebook in hand and red curls bouncing, she walked toward the car.

"Oh, Mikey, isn't she a cutie! She's so small you could just put her in your pocket."

I had forgotten to remind my mom not to do anything embarrassing like the time she saw Melissa in the book store. So I figured I'd better say something now, before Liz got into the car. Using my sternest, most serious voice I said, "Mom, please do not embarrass me when Liz gets in the car."

"What?" was all my mother could say before Liz opened the backseat door and climbed in.

"Hey," I said, as Liz buckled her seat belt. She

wore a green shirt which really brought out the green in her eyes. "Liz, this is my mom. Mom, this is Liz."

"Oh my goodness," Mom began. "Aren't you just so adorable? Mikey didn't want me to say anything to embarrass him, but you should never be embarrassed of the truth. And you are adorable."

Liz blushed. I had to find a way to stop the train wreck Mom was about to create if she kept going. "Hey, mom, we're all set. You know how to get there?"

Mom put the car in gear and ignored my comment, and began talking to Liz. "Hey Liz, do you like the Beatles?"

Oh no! There she goes. I knew what was coming next and there was no way to stop her. I made a mental note to myself. Someday when I become a parent, I'm going to be cool and never ever embarrass my kids!

Mom pushed play on the CD player and began singing along loudly, getting Liz to join her in the chorus of the song. I stared out the window, melting into my seat, wondering how this could possibly get any worse.

"Liz, do you know when Mikey was a baby, I would play this song and he would take off his clothes and dance naked all around the living room."

There it was. It officially got worse.

Chapter 48

It seemed like it took forever, but we finally pulled up to the Mason house. But this wasn't just any house, it was more like a mansion. It was large and white, with windows on all three floors, and green ivy vines clinging to the sides. Mom parked the car and Liz and I got out and walked up the brick sidewalk to a giant red door.

Liz rang the doorbell then looked at me. "Are you ready?"

"I don't have a choice at this point," I said as I heard footsteps from inside.

The door opened and an older man, dressed in shirt and tie, greeted us. "Hello, I presume you are the students here to conduct an interview with Ms.

Mason. My name is Mr. David. I am Ms. Mason's

personal assistant. Please follow me."

Liz and I stepped into the giant foyer of the

house. We followed Mr. David past a large staircase

leading upstairs and past a room that looked like a

combination of library and office. We turned and

headed down a hallway that led past a couple of closed

doors, and then through a small living room that

looked like it had never been used. We turned once

more and walked into a large sunlit porch that had a

view of the backyard and a lush garden.

Mr. David pointed to a couple of chairs.

"Would you care for a beverage?" he asked. "I have a

variety of colas and juices to offer."

I looked at Liz, wondering what Mr. David

meant by 'colas.' "Do you have any soda?" I asked.

Liz rolled her eyes and whispered to me, "Cola and soda is the same thing."

"Aren't you the bright one," Mr. David said to Liz.

"I'll have a diet soda, please," Liz said.

"Yeah, me too," I added trying to sound like I knew what I was talking about.

"Very good," Mr. David said. "Ms. Mason will be with you shortly." And he left the porch.

I waited until he was gone. "This place is huge," I began. "And she has a butler! I mean, a personal assistant, but it's the same thing as a butler. Just like cola and soda, right?"

"Yeah, I noticed that, Captain Obvious," Liz replied. She opened her notebook and began looking again at the questions we wanted to ask Ms. Mason. I know Liz wanted to sound mature and not like a little kid doing an interview.

As she was reading, I gazed out at the sunlit garden and trees. A slight wind began to stir the leaves and I noticed as the giant sunflower plants began to sway back and forth with the breeze. The wind subsided and the garden was still. Then, as if a tornado had suddenly sprang up in the middle of the garden, all of the leaves and plants began to rock furiously back and forth. A cold chill swept through the porch, causing Liz to shiver. She looked at me.

"What was that?" she asked folding her arms

for warmth.

I knew instantly what was going on. "Travis is here."

Chapter 49

I heard a noise at the doorway and turned to see Mr. David returning with our drinks. He set down two small glasses that had ice and about a quarter of a can of soda in each. I could have easily finished mine in one gulp. He stood straight up after setting the glasses down and tilted his head like a dog listening for something off in the distance. Mr. David looked out at the garden which had returned to normal just as quickly as it had started. He spoke, his eyes shifting from side to side, "I thought I felt a slight chill, but it seems better now. I'll have to have the air conditioner repairman come and take a look."

"It feels just fine out here, Mr. David," said Ms. Mason, smiling as she entered the porch. I knew she was older but I was surprised by how young her face looked.   She glided toward us. "I see you have beverages."

Mr. David realized that she did not have a drink and spoke immediately, "Tea, madam?"

"Thank you, Mr. David," Ms. Mason responded. Her eyes followed after him as he left the room. It was hard to put my finger on it, but there seemed to be something more than just an old lady and her butler going on here. I think she liked him or something, the way she was looking at him.

Ms. Mason sat across from Liz and me. While it was true that her face looked young, when she folded her hands on her lap they were definitely old and wrinkly and had lots of little brown spots. She smiled at both of us then turned to Liz. "I was so pleased to receive your call. It is so refreshing to hear about young people taking an interest in our community. And I was delighted that you chose the Mason Warehouse for your research project. For almost a century the Mason Warehouse was the backbone of this community."

"Wow," I said, mostly because I didn't know what else to say and it seemed like Ms. Mason was waiting for a response.

Liz flipped open her notebook and, looking at Ms. Mason, began, "I know your father started the business and we'll get to that in a minute. I thought we'd work our way back through time. Why don't we start with the fire? How did the warehouse get destroyed, Ms. Mason?"

Ms. Mason seemed shocked by this first question. I was definitely shocked by it. Liz was so calm and direct that she seemed more like a seasoned reporter than a sixth-grade girl. Ms. Mason's wrinkly hands began to roll back and forth over each other as she leaned back. Yes, Liz had clearly surprised her with the question.

"Your tea, madam." Mr. David was back and set the tea cup on the table. From his shifting eyes, I could tell he knew he had walked into an awkward situation. "Will that be all or would you like me to stay?"

Ms. Mason told him that she was fine and they exchanged the kind of glances that you'd expect to see in a Junior High hallway between a boy and a girl who like each other, not between an old lady and her butler. Mr. David's goo-goo eyes for Ms. Mason evaporated as he pivoted toward Liz and me with a cautionary gaze. It was the kind of look a teacher gives you when they think you might be cheating on a quiz but they haven't quite caught you. It was just starting to get kind of awkward and weird when he turned and left the porch.

Ms. Mason watched him leave, then took a sip of her tea. "The fire was a tragedy. The warehouse business was lost and two people lost their lives."

"Don't you mean three, Ms. Mason," Liz responded. "Wasn't a man executed because of the fire as well?"

I'm pretty sure my eyes about popped out of

my head when Liz came back with that. I half expected

Ms. Mason to throw us out on the spot. Instead, she

leaned forward and patted Liz's hand in a sweet

gesture. "You are so right, dear," she began. "The fire

was a tragedy on many levels. It still hurts to discuss it.

Could we possibly come back to it later? I'll tell you

what. I have a scrapbook full of pictures inside that

you might be interested in and it will give you a good

idea of what the structure looked like. Would you care

to see them?"

Liz shifted in her chair and responded just as

sweetly. "We would love to see the scrapbook,

wouldn't we, Mike?"

I was caught off guard by Liz bringing me into

this.   I wasn't sure what was going on with these two, but even I could feel the tension in the room. Suddenly, goose bumps began to appear on my arm and I felt a cold chill down my neck. I looked up over Liz's shoulder, and there in the window of the house was Travis. His pale face and red hair were dulled by the pane of glass in front of him. His face looked as angry as ever, as his hand rose up and motioned for me to come inside.

"Mike?" Liz asked again.

Startled back to the moment, I replied, "Yeah, let's go inside."

Chapter 50

Ms. Mason took us to a room she called the parlor. It looked just like another living room to me. While she and Liz were looking through the scrapbook, I was looking around for another sign from Travis. Until the breeze in the garden and seeing him in the window, it had been days since I had seen him. I knew he must be well rested and I had no idea what to expect now that we were here. But, I also knew what he was capable of, which is why I was very surprised by what happened next.

It started with a feeling of my ears beginning to get full, like when you go way down to the bottom of the pool. I couldn't shake the plugging feeling. And then in a muffled whisper, I thought I heard the word,

"Library."

I looked around quickly to see if anyone else had heard the word, but Liz and Ms. Mason were still flipping through old pictures and talking.

"Library," I heard again. It was still difficult to understand, but this time Travis said it with more urgency. It was a demand, not a request.

I stood up and interrupted Ms. Mason. "Would you mind if I looked around your library? I'm a big fan of old books and it looked like you had a lot in there." I know it was lame, but that was the best excuse I could manage.

Ms. Mason wrinkled her brow in suspicion. I know she was wondering what I might be up to. Then, once again, in a sweet voice she told me to go ahead and be her guest. Liz looked at me with surprise and, with her eyes, warned me to be careful. I didn't need a warning.

THEY CALL ME ZOMBIE

Chapter 51

I walked back down the hallway until I found the small room that served as an office and library. My ears had begun to return to normal again, but as soon as I walked into the room, I could tell by the chill that Travis was there. I stood inside and gazed at the three walls filled with shelves of books. In front of one wall was an antique looking desk with assorted papers and books on it.

I began to walk along one wall, looking at the large collection of books. Most of the titles and authors I had never even heard of. Some of them I couldn't even pronounce. I finished the first wall and as I scanned the books behind the desk, I saw my nemesis, *Tom Sawyer*. I hated that book. I continued on to the last wall. There must have been hundreds of books there. In all, I only knew four of the titles, and I had read none of them.

I returned to the middle of the room. I had no idea what Travis wanted me to do here and just as I was wondering, I felt my ears fill with pressure again.

Muffled words sounding like someone trying to talk underwater filled my ears. This was something new. Travis was apparently a ghost of very few words, but when he had spoken to me in the past, I seemed able to understand him most of the time.

I shook my head back and forth, trying to release the pressure. It sounded like he said 'top drawer,' but I couldn't be sure. The pressure became greater, almost to the point of hurting. I put my hands to my ears and again, the muffled sound of "top drawer" filled my head.

I made my way to the large desk and sat down in the brown leather chair. I looked back to the doorway to be sure the coast was clear. Reaching down with both hands, I began to pull on the old wooden drawer. It creaked loudly in the quiet room and moved slightly, but did not open. I tried again. More creaks and groans, but the drawer still would not open and I realized that it was locked.

Gazing around the desk I saw a letter opener, which is basically a small dull knife that old people use to open letters. Don't ask me why. I reached for it and slid it into the small space between the desk and the drawer and moved it back and forth until I heard a click.

I set the letter opener down and the drawer easily slid open in my hands. On the left side I saw pens and pencils and paperclips. On the right side were papers. I picked up the one on top and opened it. It was a bank statement for Ms. Mason. My jaw almost hit the desk when I saw the amount of money in her account. Even after all of the years since the fire, she was still a millionaire.

My breath came out in a mist over the paper. The temperature had dropped dramatically. I glanced up to see Travis standing just a few feet from the desk. I know he saved me from Craig in the bathroom, but the look on his face terrified me as much as anything I had ever seen from him. He was pointing at me and his chest was heaving in anger. I didn't understand. What was he trying to tell me?

With shaky hands, I held the paper up to show him what I had found. This only seemed to infuriate him even more. His black eyes fixed on mine.

"NO," I heard him scream loud and clear. Then he rushed toward me. Instinctively, I ducked below the desk and felt a freezing blast of air go past me, knocking papers from the desk on top of me.

"What do you think you're doing?"

I popped my head up above the desk and there stood Mr. David. His eyes scanned the room as if he suspected that someone else might be in there with us. After slowly inspecting the room, his gaze fell upon me.

"What do you think you are doing," he repeated sternly.

"Oh," I stumbled up from the floor, paper still in hand. "Ms. Mason said I could come in here and look at the books." I knew that wasn't good enough. I needed to think of something quick. "I sneezed and I must have knocked over some of the papers... so I was picking them up."

Mr. David looked at me suspiciously as I set the paper back onto the desk and leaned in with my thigh to slowly close the drawer. I bent down and picked up the remaining papers and placed them in a pile on the desk. Mr. David stared at me and I nervously looked around the room in the awkward silence.

"There are a lot of nice books here. I like

books. I like to read. Have you read all of these?"

More silence. "I think I'll go back and check on Liz." I

said as I walked past Mr. David's threatening eyes.

Chapter 52

I returned to find Liz and Ms. Mason just finishing up. Mr. David, who had followed me back to the parlor, walked us to the front door. We walked quietly down the sidewalk until we reached the street. Liz turned to me.

"What was going on? Did you find anything?" she asked.

"I heard Travis tell me to go to the library. You and Ms. Mason were right there but you guys acted like you didn't hear a sound." I said.

"Well that's because we didn't hear anything." Liz said flatly. She looked at me impatiently, waiting to hear what else had happened.

"I went to the library and Travis told me to look in the top drawer of the desk. I got it open and found Ms. Mason's bank statement. She's loaded. She has millions. Anyways, Travis appeared and was about as angry as I've ever seen him so I must have grabbed the wrong paper. Next thing I knew, there were papers blowing all over the place and Mr. David was standing in the room asking what I was doing."

Liz turned back to the house. "She's hiding something. I asked her two more times about the fire, but she didn't want to talk about it. Mike, I think she set the fire. I can't prove it, but I've just got this feeling that she did it. Why else would Travis lead us here?"

I couldn't prove it either, but I had a feeling that Liz was right. And if she was right, that meant that I would have to go back into the house and get back in

the drawer to find what Travis wanted me to find.

Chapter 53

Monday was back to school. I hooked up with Tom and Rosie at lunch. I had decided that when this thing was over, I would tell them about what was going on. I'd have to tell Rosie first, because I think I'd have a better chance of him believing me. In the meantime, it was safer for everyone if only a couple of people knew.

After lunch I went to my locker to grab my notebook for English. I had just popped open the door when a large hand slammed it shut from behind me, almost crushing my hand inside. I turned and it was one of Craig's bully sidekicks.

"Hey Zombie-Boy," he said moving into my space. This was the sidekick who looked most like a caveman. He already had hair growing on his face and where most people have two separate eyebrows, he had one long one. As he began talking all I could do was stare at the uni-brow.

"So, listen, I have a message from Craig. He said he wants to meet with you after school. Just the two of you. To talk. Meet him outside the gym. Don't show up and he'll kill you."

The caveman and his one long eyebrow bumped into my shoulder as he walked away. I opened my locker back up. Great, I can go and meet Craig and get beat up or I can hide from Craig and get beat up. So many super choices!

I closed my locker and headed to English class wondering what I should do and if this day could get any worse. I took my seat and got my answer from the teacher.

"Good afternoon. We're going to start a new novel today. It's a classic adventure tale by one of our great American authors. I think you're really going to enjoy, *Tom Sawyer*."

Chapter 54

I watched and waited as the clock ticked down to the end of the day. I had decided to meet Craig outside the gym. Whatever was going to happen, I just wanted to get it over with.

As I walked around the corner of the building I saw him. He looked even bigger than the last time I had seen him. He was wearing a tan t-shirt and his hair was swept back making him look like a lion. I walked over and stopped about three feet away, thinking to myself that would give me room to try to make a run if I needed to. I imagined it would look like something from one of those nature shows where a little gazelle tries to outrun a lion. And we all know how that ends for the gazelle.

"Come here," Craig started pointing to a cement bench nearby. "Sit down."

I took one step forward, then stopped. My heart was racing as I was trying to be brave.

"I'm not going to hit you," Craig said as he sat down on the bench.

I knew that he could have already pummeled me if he had wanted to. I walked cautiously to the bench and sat down.

Craig leaned forward and began to speak without looking at me, "Here's the deal. I asked Melissa to the dance last night and she told me she was already going with someone else. I know it's you." Craig leaned back and turned toward me. "The only reason she's interested in you is because she feels sorry for you because you were dead. Seriously, why else would a hot girl like her be interested in you?"

I had wondered that myself several times.

"So here's what's going to happen. I know you've been hanging around that pixie girl…what's her name?"

"Liz?" I asked.

"Yeah, whatever. She seems nice and I think you two make a great pair. So what you're going to do is ask your little pixie to the dance and tell Melissa that you already have a date. I'll take Melissa and everyone wins. You have a date, I have a date, and best of all, you don't get your butt kicked."

I had to admit that there was a sort of logic to

what Craig had said. Knowing that, I couldn't believe what came out of my mouth. "If Melissa liked you, she would have asked you to the dance."

Craig stood up and took a deep breath. I'm pretty sure he wanted to clobber me right on the spot, but he slowly let the air out of his lungs and folded his massive arms. "That's the deal, Zombie. If you show up at the dance Friday night with Melissa, it'll be the last dance you ever go to."

Chapter 55

When I got home and walked into the kitchen, all of the drawers and cupboards were open. It wasn't cold in the house so I knew Travis wasn't there at the moment, but it was clearly evident that he had been here, and was not happy.

"Thanks a lot, Travis," I said as I began closing all of the open drawers and cupboard doors. "I know I messed up at the Mason house. Sorry about that. I have to tell you, though, you've done this kitchen thing before, and it's not as scary as the first time. If you want to do something really scary, try cleaning my room."

I knew I would probably regret saying that last comment. The last thing I really wanted to do was

make an angry, scary ghost even angrier and scarier.
But think about it, I have a ghost problem, a bully
problem and girl problems. I have a lot going on and
it's starting to wear on me.

I closed the last drawer and leaned against the
counter. "Sorry about that room comment, Travis," I
added and then mumbled, "Although it would be
pretty cool if you could clean it for me."

The silence of the kitchen was broken by Tom's
familiar voice, "Hey, any dead people live here?"

I walked to the front door and there were Tom
and Rosie standing outside the screened door. "Hold
on guys." I walked back to the kitchen to grab some
popsicles, then I went outside and we sat on the steps.

Tom took a lick of his popsicle and said, "Mikey,

285

it's all over the school that if you show up to the dance with Melissa, Craig is going to pop you like a pimple."

"I'm a little worried about you, Mikey." Rosie began in between licks of his purple popsicle. "What are you going to do?"

"I don't know." I replied. The truth was I really didn't know. I liked Melissa and I liked Liz. I really didn't want to get beaten up by Craig, but I didn't want to back down from him either. I wondered why this all had to be so complicated.

Tom was already halfway through his popsicle before he noticed it was orange and complained, "Really? The orange one again?"

"I know the right thing for you to do is to follow your heart," said Rosie. "What's your heart telling you?"

Tom coughed loudly choking on his popsicle. "Did you really just say that? Do you go home and watch *Oprah* all day? What kind of advice is that?" Tom scoffed.

"Hey," Rosie interjected, "I'm a romantic."

"Are you guys going to the dance?" I asked, trying to change the subject.

"Yeah," Tom replied.

Rosie scooted over next to Tom, leaned his head on Tom's shoulder and in a high pitched voice asked, "Will you dance with me?"

Tom tried to shove him away but Rosie wasn't an easy kid to move. "Get away from me." Tom complained. "First I get the stupid orange popsicle again and now I've got you practically sitting on my lap! What's wrong with you two?"

Rosie stood up and began an exaggerated dance, swinging his arms wildly back and forth and his head from side to side. In a sing song voice he belted out, "All the ladies want to dance with Rosie, all the ladies and Tom!"

I burst out laughing. It was the hardest and loudest I had laughed in a long time.

Chapter 56

After the guys left I made some mac and cheese and played some video games. I started getting bored and then I started thinking that maybe I should clean the kitchen before my mom got home. Thinking of cleaning reminded me of Mrs. Grey, which made me think maybe I should call her. There was a lot of thinking going on when my cell phone rang. It was Mrs. Grey.

"Hey, Mrs. Grey. How did you know I was thinking about calling you?" I asked jokingly.

"I didn't know that, Michael." Mrs. Grey responded in a serious tone. "I'm calling you because I'm afraid I have some news that may not be very pleasant. My grandmother had a vision today. In the vision she saw a young man. He was in an old, white house with a brick walkway. Inside he was standing in a small room full of books and she sensed great danger there for him. Does that mean anything to you, Michael?"

I swallowed hard as chills ran down my spine. "I was already in that room Mrs. Grey." I told her what had happened at the Mason house and I told her how I had messed up and had to go back.

"I don't think you should go Michael." Mrs. Grey warned.

I couldn't help it, but I snapped at Mrs. Grey. "I don't want to go back! But whatever Travis needs to prove his innocence is in that house and in that room. Ms. Mason must have set that fire and apparently the evidence is in that desk drawer. And if I recall correctly, you're the one who has been telling me all along to just ask it what it wants. Well, I've been doing that and it's pretty clear that what Travis wants is in that desk. And I'm afraid of what will happen if I don't help him out. So now I have no choice. I have to go back."

I was scared and angry and I took it out on Mrs. Grey. There was a long pause on the other end of the line. I didn't mean to make Mrs. Grey feel bad, but it was her advice that led me this far.

"How do you plan to get back in?" Mrs. Grey asked.

"I don't know yet but, Liz and I are working on a plan."

"Is Liz the short, cute girl with green eyes?" she asked.

"Yeah, how did you know? Did your grandmother see her in the vision, too?" I worried.

"No Michael, you told me about her last time we talked."

"Oh."

There was another long pause before Mrs. Grey spoke again. "Grandmother's visions are not wrong, Michael. There is danger waiting for you in that house. You must promise me that, once you have a plan, you will call me. If you need my help, I will go with you."

Now I really felt guilty about making Mrs. Grey feel bad. Mrs. Grey was willing to risk her life to go with me. "I'll be okay," I told her. "As soon as I know what the plan is, I promise to call you."

Mrs. Grey said goodnight and hung up the phone. It was the first time that she hadn't had some sort of comment for me. Usually she would end our talks with some snappy words of wisdom that made me wish I had thought of them first. The fact that she was worried made me worried. Was there something waiting for me in that house more dangerous than bullies or ghosts?

Chapter 57

The next three days were pretty quiet. Liz was out of school sick, so I was left trying to organize our information by myself. Even with everything going on, we still had a project that was due next week. Although I hadn't seen Craig or his goons, at least three people a day asked me if I was going to the dance with Melissa.

When I got home from school that day, Liz was waiting for me on the steps. I was surprised but happy to see her. "What are you doing here? You're supposed to be sick."

"I'm feeling better, so my mom let me come over for a bit. I'll be back in school tomorrow." She said. "Thanks for your texts by the way. It gets boring sitting at home all day just watching TV or reading."

"No problem," I replied. "I know what it's like to be home alone all day. Actually, I guess most days I wasn't alone because Travis was there, but I know what you mean."

Liz smiled and slid over so I could sit down. She pushed a strand of curly hair away from her eyes and whispered, "I have a plan."

"What is it?" I asked, scared and excited at the same time.

"I called Ms. Mason again. I told her that we had forgotten to get a picture of her for the project and I asked if I could come back to take one. She said yes." Liz paused, "We set it up for tomorrow night at seven."

"Where do I fit into this?" I asked.

"I've got a plan to distract Mr. David. Once I get into the house, I'll find a way to meet you at the porch door and let you in the back. Then I'll keep Ms. Mason busy. You'll have a few minutes to get into the library, get what you're looking for, and get out."

I rubbed my hands on my head. "Despite the fact that your plan is full of holes, I don't even know what I'm looking for. What if I can't find it in a few minutes?"

"You were obviously close last time. You've got to do it. This is the only shot we're going to get." Liz stood up, took a few steps and turned around. "If it all goes well, we'll be in and out in a few minutes and you'll be on your way to the dance."

Since I hadn't seen her in a few days, I wasn't sure if Liz knew about what was going on. I stood up, "Look," I began, "I was going to tell you…"

Liz interrupted me with a calm voice, "It's okay, Mikey. The prettiest girl in the whole school asked you out. You'd be stupid not to go. I understand." She turned and began walking down the sidewalk.

"Liz," I called out to her.

"Just be ready for tomorrow night." She said as she walked away.

Chapter 58

Friday was the longest day of my life. Every class seemed to drag and the more I watched the clock, the slower it seemed to move. It was like everything was in slow motion. On top of that, Craig and his goons made sure to remind me that tonight was the dance. The uni-brow goon was leaning on the wall across from my locker in the morning, arms folded, just watching me. The other one was waiting for me outside math class. He followed slowly behind me for a while, then disappeared in the crowded hall. And Craig was waiting in the lobby, outside of the lunch room. I tried not to look at him, but I could feel his eyes glaring at me. Each time I looked over, he was still glaring at me, his lips curled into a barely noticeable smile. None of them said a word. They all just stared at me. Silent intimidation.

I saw Melissa after gym class and she told me that she would meet me at the dance tonight. I told her I might be a little late and she was fine with that. There was no way I could tell her my reason. How do you explain that you're going to be breaking into a house to help a ghost? You just don't.

Liz found me at the end of the day and told me that our plan had hit a snag. "We don't have a ride there," she explained. "My mom's car is in the shop and she won't have it back until tomorrow."

"I'm on it!" I exclaimed. "Meet at my house at 6:30 and we'll go from there."

I called Mrs. Grey and even though she'd offered to help, she was hesitant. She reminded me of her grandmother's vision and she said she wasn't very sure about our plan. When I asked her if she had a better idea, there was silence. Finally, after what seemed like an hour, she hummed, and agreed to give us a ride.

I got home after school, threw my backpack on the floor and made a snack. I tried to picture the small library in my mind and the top drawer. Whatever I was looking for must have been in the small stack of papers inside. Should I look through them or just grab them all and run? I'd have to decide that when I got there.

At six I went upstairs to my room. I stood wondering what to wear, not to the dance but for the break-in. I had never been to a break-in before. I picked out a pair of dark blue jeans and a black hoodie.

Wearing dark clothes seemed to make sense. As I got changed I felt a slight cool breeze filter through my room. I looked around waiting for the temperature to drop further or to see Travis, but neither happened.

I went back to the kitchen and grabbed a small pen-sized flashlight from the junk drawer. I turned it on and no light. I banged it twice in my hand, the light popped on and I put it in my pocket. I stood looking around wondering if there was anything else I might need, but nothing came to mind.

At six-thirty, the doorbell rang. As I was opening the door for Liz, Mrs. Grey pulled up out front. Liz and I walked to the car and in a moment we were off. The ride was silent. As I stared out the window at the passing houses, I began to wonder about Mrs.

Grey's grandmother's warning. I had tried not to think about it, but now, I was just minutes away from the Mason house. I bit my lip and tried to convince myself that maybe not all of her visions came true.

Chapter 59

Mrs. Grey dropped us off a block away from the house. "Be careful, the both of you," she warned us with worried eyes. "If anything goes wrong, I will be right here. If you are not back in ten minutes, then I will call the police and come looking for you."

Liz and I got out and walked down the darkened street. She stopped at the row of bushes just before the house. "I'll meet you at the back door in a couple of minutes." Before I could respond, Liz leaned up and kissed me on the cheek. "Good luck," she whispered. Then she turned with determination and was off down the street toward the house.

I waited until she began to walk down the brick sidewalk, then I snuck between the bushes and into the backyard. I made my way through the evening

shadows of the garden and crouched, waiting outside

the porch door.

Liz was greeted at the door by Mr. David and

escorted once again into the parlor.

"It's so nice to see you again," said Ms. Mason,

as she walked into the room. "I'm sorry your little

friend wasn't able to join you."

"Yeah, he had a dance to go to," Liz responded.

"Well, shall we get this picture taking over

with?" asked Ms. Mason as she sat down in a high-

backed chair, already beginning to pose.

"Can I use your bathroom first?" Liz asked, as

she started to leave the room. "I know where it is I'll

just be a minute."

I heard the latch for the porch door click and Liz pushed the door open, nodded at me, then went back into the house.

I stood, carefully opened the door and entered the porch. I heard the house doorbell ring and I knew Mr. David would be going to answer the door. I snuck down the hallway toward the library and from the corner, was able to see part of the conversation as Mr. David answered the front door.

"Hello?"

"Hi. It's Pete's Pizza," began the thirty-year-old deliver boy in the baggy brown pants. "If it says Pete's, it's got to be Pizza. I've got eight large pizzas for Mr. David."

"I did not order any pizza," Mr. David responded dryly.

"Sure you did," said the delivery boy, "Look here, I've got pepperoni, I've got sausage, I've got Hawaiian…"

"I can assure you that I did not order pizza," Mr. David interrupted.

"Listen, Bubo, I got a slip of paper here that says eight pizzas for Mr. David at this address." The delivery boy responded.

I slipped into the library and carefully closed the door behind me. Liz's plan was great. I would have loved to have stayed and listened to the rest of that argument, but I had work to do. I hoped that Liz was still safe as I clicked on my small flashlight and walked to the desk.

Chapter 60

I slipped into the chair behind the desk and pulled gently on the top drawer. I expected it to be locked, but it slowly creaked open in my hands. I placed the flashlight in my mouth so I could use both hands. I saw that in a spy movie once and I thought it was pretty cool. I immediately found the stack of papers on the right side and, with no idea of what I was looking for, began going through them.

A cold rush of breeze blew across my hands and the temperature in the room instantly dropped. I looked up to see Travis standing on the other side of the desk. His black eyes were sharp and his head was cocked slightly to one side. His face contorted into a look of anger and frustration. "NOOO," came his whispery growl.

My ears began to fill again as Travis spoke.

"Top drawer," he said, in a muffled rage.

I raised my hands as if to ask 'what am I looking for?' He clenched his teeth, then spoke again.

"*Tom Sawyer*," he said pointing at me.

I sat back in shock. Did he just say *Tom Sawyer* I wondered? "Did you just say Tom Sawyer?" I asked aloud.

Travis moved his head up and down, pointed and repeated, "*Tom Sawyer*."

I turned to look at the bookshelf behind me, and there at eye level was the book. I pulled it from the shelf and showed it to Travis. "This?"

Travis clenched his fists and nodded his head again. "Yes," he said in a breathy whisper.

I looked down at the book and back up again, but Travis was gone. All along I thought Travis had been saying 'top drawer' when he had really been saying '*Tom Sawyer*!' No wonder he was so angry! But what did this book have to do with anything? I turned back toward the bookshelf to keep the light away from the door and opened the book. I knew in seconds that this was not *Tom Sawyer*. Inside was a hand written diary, with dates and entries starting fifteen years ago. The first page of the book listed a date and the author's name: Kyle David.

Flashlight in my mouth, I flipped through pages until the book fell open to an entry dated March of

1998.

"It didn't have to be this way but they left me no choice. I had to protect Linda. If I allowed those men to close the warehouse, Linda would have been bankrupt and destroyed. I tried to reason with them one last time, when they refused, I poisoned them and set the warehouse on fire. With the insurance policy, Linda will have millions and someday we will be together. She has no idea how much I love her. Someday, years from now, she'll know."

I sat in stunned silence. It wasn't Ms. Mason who set the fire. It was Mr. David.

Chapter 61

If Mr. David set the fire, then he must have also set up Travis to take the blame. I flipped further into the diary looking for more evidence. In the back of my mind I was thinking that maybe getting hit by the *Tom Sawyer* book, twice, and having to read it in English class were not just coincidences.

As I was turning pages in the diary another thought occurred to me. I found what I was looking for. I should get out of here. Now!

Suddenly a hand grabbed me by the back of my hoodie, pulled me to my feet and spun me around. "Just what do you think you're doing," snarled Mr. David.

The flashlight, still in my mouth, illuminated his

face in an eerie glow. He'd seemed so proper and

snobby before, now he appeared menacing and

deadly. "Give me that book," he ordered.

    Instinctively, I put it behind my back and held

on tight. Mr. David pulled me close, then shoved me

with a surprising force sending me crashing into the

bookshelf and onto the floor. The flashlight fell from

my mouth and turned off, leaving the room in

complete blackness. I held the diary with one hand,

and with my free hand, I scrambled to find the light. I

felt it roll between my fingers, slip away, and then I

found it again. I banged it against my leg and the light

popped back on.

    Mr. David was standing by the desk, the letter

opener in his hand like a knife. "Give me that book

now," he growled.   As he spoke his breath came out in mist and I noticed the temperature turned freezing again.

Mr. David stepped toward me, knife raised to strike. Without warning, a book flew from the shelf above me, just missing Mr. David's head, instead crashing into the wall behind him.

"What the devil?" he asked, in stunned surprise.

Another larger book flew from the shelf and hit him squarely in the face with a solid thump, knocking him a couple of steps backward. Book after book began flying from the shelf striking Mr. David and creating soaring shadows on the ceiling. The letter opener fell from his hand as he tried to shield himself from the barrage of flying books. Each book that hit

him struck harder than the one before. In the dim

glow of the flashlight I saw books begin circling the

room then leaving the chain to fly furiously at Mr.

David, coming at him from all directions now. Thud

after thud echoed in the room as the books continued

to pummel him. Slowly, he crumpled to the floor,

whimpering under the pounding of the books.

Chapter 62

The library door exploded inward as two uniformed police officers burst into the room. At the same moment, all of the books circling above fell to the floor in a dull thud. The female police officer flipped on the light and they both gazed around at the destruction of the room.

"Whoa!" exclaimed the other officer, "What the heck happened in here?"

Liz pushed past the two cops and knelt by my side. Behind her I saw Ms. Mason and Mrs. Grey standing in the doorway.

"You're bleeding," Liz said, as she pulled a tissue from her pocket and wiped away a streak of blood from my mouth. "Are you okay?"

"It was Mr. David," I said as I pulled the diary out from behind my back. "Mr. David set the warehouse fire. Mr. David killed the two men inside and Mr. David set up Travis Cleveland Riley to take the blame. It's all in here."

The female police officer took the diary from me and began flipping through it.

"Kyle, what's the meaning of this?" Ms. Mason asked, clearly confused.

Mr. David brushed away books from his battered and bruised body. His face was darkened and reddened from the pounding of the books. "I did it for you, Linda," he pleaded, trying to explain. "I did it for you. You would have been broke, you would have lost everything. I love you."

Ms. Mason's trembling hands went up to her pale face. "Kyle, what have you done?" she asked, tears welling up in her eyes. Shocked by the realization that Mr. David was responsible for all of the terrible events surrounding the warehouse, she suddenly looked so much older and fragile. As she began to weep, Mrs. Grey wrapped an arm around her and gently led her away from the room.

The female police officer handed the diary to her partner, pulled out her handcuffs and helped Mr. David to his feet. "Sir, you're under arrest."

She led him from the room reading him his rights. Mr. David's words, "I did it for you, Linda," echoed in the hallway as she led him out of the house.

The other police officer, Officer Brown, gazed

down at me. "You okay, kid?" he asked.

"I'm fine," I responded, still stunned by all that had happened.

He held the book up for me to see and said, "Good job!" Then he left the room.

"You did it!" Liz exclaimed.

"We did it," I replied. I gazed around at the cluttered piles of books and added, "With a little help from Travis."

Chapter 63

Once we got outside, Officer Brown had Liz and I walk over to his car to get our names and addresses and to ask some more questions while Mrs. Grey hovered a short distance away.

After what seemed like ten-thousand questions, he flipped his note pad closed, "I've got what I need for now. You two hop in the backseat and I'll take you home and try to explain this to your parents."

Liz and I, mouths open and eyes pleading, looked to Mrs. Grey for help.

Hands fidgeting, she stepped forward. "Excuse me Officer, ah, Brown is it? Yes, hmmm, I am the grandmother. I am the grandmother of the children so

I will be taking them home."

Officer Brown's forehead wrinkled and he regarded Mrs. Grey with some doubt. "Your last name is Grey," he began, "they've got two different last names. How are you the grandmother?"

Mrs. Grey, momentarily surprised, faked a cough and then began one of the longest made-up stories I've ever heard. "Well, you see Officer Brown. It's really quite a charming story. Shortly after my mother was married, her father, my grandfather, lived just down the street in a lovely colonial. It was white and blue and he grew the most beautiful daisies that lined a cobblestone walkway that led to the house."

Mrs. Grey went on and on, in excruciating detail, describing the house and the daisies. Then she started describing the neighbor's house and the daisies they had in their yard. Finally, Officer Brown had heard enough and interrupted in an exasperated tone, "Listen lady, I've got three hours of paper work waiting for me back at the station. Just take the kids home."

On the ride back with Mrs. Grey and Liz, I explained everything that had happened from the moment I entered the porch. Liz talked about how she pretended to not know how to use the camera and purposely messing up the pictures to keep Ms. Mason occupied. Mrs. Grey said that Ms. Mason had no idea that Mr. David had set the fires and that she was devastated.

The ride went quickly and, before I knew it, Mrs. Grey brought the car to a stop outside of the school. The dance! I had forgotten all about it. I looked at Mrs. Grey, then at Liz.

"You're lip is still swollen," Liz said. "You might want to think of a reason to explain it before Melissa asks you what happened," she added.

"I don't have to go." I said.

"Yes, you do," Liz responded. "Text me tomorrow sometime and we'll figure out a time to get together. We still have a project to finish up this weekend."

I opened the door and got out of the car and watched as Mrs. Grey and Liz drove off.

Chapter 64

Loud, thumping music and spiraling lights greeted me as I walked into the gym. There was a large group of kids dancing and pockets of other kids scattered about in small groups around the outside of the gym and at the snack tables.

I saw Melissa standing off to one side with her friends Brenda and Jennica. She glowed like a movie star in the sparking lights. Her long blond hair flowed off her shoulders onto her dress. She could easily be a model I thought. I stood just watching for a moment.

Finally, I took a deep breath and walked across the gym. Melissa's face lit up when she saw me. "Mikey, you made it!" As I got closer, she raised her hand to my face, "What happened to your lip?"

"Ahhh?" I had forgotten to think of an excuse. "I fell going down the stairs?"

"Oh, I hope it doesn't hurt too much." She replied.

After an awkward moment she asked, "Do you want to dance?"

I gazed out at the gym full of dancing kids and then back to Melissa. "Can we talk for a minute first?" I asked.

Melissa reached for my hand and held it as she led me out of the gym and into the coolness of the hallway. We turned down the hall and walked down to the main corridor and sat on a bench.

I swallowed hard. "You look amazing by the

way."

Melissa smiled, "Thanks, Mikey."

"Listen, I just wanted to ask you something." I began. I could feel my palms getting sweaty. "Why me? I mean you are the most beautiful girl in the school. You could go to the dance with any guy you want. And I'm, well, I'm just me. I don't understand it?"

Melissa smiled and held my hand again, making me even more nervous. "It's simple," she said. "Do you know how many guys chase me around? Do you know how often they say stupid things trying to be clever or to impress me? I like you because you don't do those things. You're nice and funny and I feel like I can be myself around you. When you jumped into the pool to splash me that was awesome, most guys wouldn't do that."

"Probably most guys don't break their neck and die doing it," I responded.

She paused, "I'm not sure what it is, but I just have this feeling that there is something special about you."

I wasn't sure what to say. I didn't know what to expect, but I wasn't expecting this.

Melissa tilted her head and continued, "I know you've been hanging out with Liz a lot lately," she said. "Do you like her? I would understand if you did. She's cute and sweet and smart. Is that why you weren't sure about coming to the dance with me?"

I didn't get the chance to answer because from over Melissa's shoulder I could see the dark, hulking figure of Craig walking toward us down the hall.

I didn't get the chance to answer because from over Melissa's shoulder I could see the dark, hulking figure of Craig walking toward us down the hall.

328

Chapter 65

"Alright, Zombie, get up." Craig snarled.

Melissa jumped up, her hands on her hips. "Leave him alone, Craig."

"This is between me and the Zombie," he replied.

I stood up and stepped toward Craig. "Listen, Craig," I began, hoping to reason my way out of a fight. "I think if we just think about this and talk it through…"

Before I could finish my sentence I felt Craig's fist hit my eye. The punch sent me sprawling across the smooth hallway floor. You know in cartoons when one of the characters gets hit and you see stars circling their head? Well, I actually saw stars when his fist hit my face. And I was surprised by how far the punch had knocked me back.   I must have slid ten feet on the smoothly waxed floor. It probably looked a lot cooler than it felt.

Melissa ran to my side and helped me to sit up. Looking at my face, she turned with anger toward my attacker. "Leave him alone, Craig!" she demanded.

"Yeah, leave him alone," came another voice.

With my one good eye, I looked over behind Craig to see Rosie, Tom and Craig's sister Brenda. Rosie and Tom stepped in between Craig and me. Rosie puffed up his chest and repeated his warning, "Leave him alone."

"What are you two going to do about it?" Craig growled.

"Jennica went to get a teacher, Craig," Brenda interjected, "I think you'd better leave."

With help from Melissa I got to my feet and stood by Rosie and Tom, face to face with Craig. I had a new surge of confidence because my two best friends in the world were there to help me. Sure, if Craig wanted to, he could still mop the floor with us, but we'd go down together.

Craig looked to his sister and then back to me. "This isn't over, Zombie." He glared at Melissa, then turned and walked out of the building.

Chapter 66

After explaining to the teacher that I had fallen down the steps- yes I used that excuse again- I got an ice pack from the nurse's office and returned to the dance. Word of 'the fight' had spread, and the fact that I had returned to the dance, black eye and all, somehow made me a hero. I didn't quite understand it, but I wasn't about to complain.

Melissa looked after my eye for a bit, told everyone how brave I was, and then asked me to dance again. She convinced Brenda and Jennica to dance with Tom and Rosie, too. Rosie was having the time of his life and doing all kinds of crazy dance moves that made us laugh. Tom and Brenda scowled more like they were waiting to get their teeth drilled in the dentist's office, but they danced anyway.

The last song was a slow song. Rosie and Jennica danced and, even though Rosie was much shorter than Jennica, they made a cute pair. Tom and Brenda stood off to the side, arms folded, waiting for the song to end. Melissa and I danced together in the center of the floor.

"Thanks for sticking up for me earlier," I said. "I think you were the brave one."

Melissa smiled at me, "Thanks for giving me a chance."

Before I knew it, the song and the dance had ended. I walked Melissa out to her mom's waiting car and she gave me a kiss on the cheek before she got in.

Rosie, Tom and I walked home together in the cool, dark night.

"What a great night," Rosie began. "There was romance in the air."

Tom looked at Rosie with disgust. "My favorite part was when Mike stopped Craig's fist with his face."

"Yeah, about that," I began, "thank you guys for saving my life back there. If it wasn't for you, I think Craig would have crushed me."

"That's what friends are for, Mikey," Rosie said putting his hand on my shoulder. "We'll always have your back."

"I'm really worried about you two," Tom said.

Chapter 67

I walked into my house and found my mom asleep on the couch, still in her work clothes. I turned off the television and covered her with a blanket. She snuggled under its warmth.

"How was your dance, Sweetie?" She mumbled, still half asleep.

"It was good, Mom," I whispered.

"That's nice, Mikey. I'll see you in the morning. I love you."

I tucked the blanket in around her and whispered, "Love you, too."

I walked up the stairs and into my room. I sat on the edge of my bed, thinking about everything that had happened today. It didn't even seem real. If it hadn't really happened, I would never have believed it.

Suddenly, the room became ice cold. I slid back on my bed and looked around my room. In the far corner a faded shadow turned into a dull light, and then into Travis. The usual angry and terrifying expression was gone, replaced by a face that seemed calm and gentle. It was strange to see, since all I had ever seen from Travis had frightened me.

"Thank you," he said in a whispery tone. His head tilted slightly to the side and for the first time his lips slowly curled into a delicate smile.

Travis began to dull and seemed to be fading away. I jumped from my bed, sparked by a memory that made my chest feel tight. "Travis," I asked. "Have you seen my Dad?"

The image of Travis continued to fade, then glowed brightly for just a split second.

"Hope." He whispered. And then he was gone.

Chapter 68

When I woke up I checked my swollen eye in the mirror. The swelling had gone down quite a bit and the skin around it had turned a dark purple. Mom was working for a half-day today, so I wouldn't have to tell her I fell down the stairs for another couple of hours. As I inspected the tender wound, I wondered what Travis had meant by "Hope" when I asked him about my Dad. I was upset that I didn't think of asking him earlier. I wondered if ghosts knew other ghosts. I wondered if my Dad was one.

After breakfast, I called Mrs. Grey, to thank her for all of her help. I told her all about the dance and about Travis's last visit. It was easy to talk to Mrs. Grey and I wondered if we would keep in touch.

"What about Liz?" she asked. "I was rather impressed with her. She seems to be an exceptional young lady."

"I know," I replied. "All of this is really confusing me. With everything that's happened I've got two girls who, for some unknown reason, seem to like me. And, I'm pretty sure I still have a bully who wants to beat me like a piñata. The only good news is that at least I'm all done with ghosts."

Mrs. Grey hummed the way she did when she knew something I didn't. After a pause she said, "Michael, this really has been quite an adventure, hasn't it? I can say this only because I've seen your writing, but if you were a better writer, I would tell you to write a book."

I could picture Mrs. Grey smiling at her little joke.

"I have to go now, Michael. Remember to call me anytime you want. And as for the young ladies, don't be in a hurry to decide anything. You have your whole life in front of you." Mrs. Grey advised, then hung up the phone.

Chapter 69

The next couple of weeks were a return to normal. It had been a long time since I had anything normal going on in my life, so it was kind of nice.

The newspaper ran a story on the arrest of Mr. David, who had confessed to setting the Mason Warehouse on fire and killing two people inside. They also printed a short article clearing Travis Cleveland Riley of any wrong doing. There never was an explanation as to why Mr. David hid his diary in a *Tom Sawyer* book cover. And, there was no mention of two brave sixth-grade students who broke into the Mason house and found the evidence. Oh well.

Liz and I finished our social studies project and got an A on it. We argued for an A+ but to no avail.

Mrs. Perkins thought it was a strange coincidence that we had done our project on the warehouse and the police had made a new arrest in the case. Liz and I agreed that it was a strange coincidence indeed. Liz and I continued to talk everyday in class and sometimes after school in the library.

Melissa and I finally went on a real date to the movies. She wanted to go and see a scary ghost movie but I talked her into a comedy. Somehow she had convinced Craig and his goons to leave me alone. That lasted about a week. After Craig found out about the movie date, he shoved my face into my locker and threatened to set a new record for how far he could knock me down the hall with one punch. So I still spend a lot of my time trying to avoid Craig and the goon squad.

I am still very confused about Liz and Melissa. I mean they're both great, but in different ways. I know it's probably tough to feel sorry for me when I've got two girls who think I'm pretty cool, but sometimes I liked it better when there were no girls. I didn't have to worry about hurting someone's feelings then.

I hadn't seen or spoken to Mrs. Grey in a couple of weeks. There were several times I thought that I should call her to say hi, but it seems like something always came up and I would forget. I wondered how she was doing and oddly enough, I missed talking to her.

I had not seen Travis since the night in my room when he thanked me. I did not miss him. I was more relieved than anything else, to have helped Travis and to have him out of my life. Except for the last visit, he had scared me every single time. I know it may sound exciting, but it's a terrible thing to wonder every waking moment of the day if a ghost is about to show up. I spend a lot of time alone at my house. Ever since this started, every little sound, every misplaced object, every time the breeze from an open window would gently move the curtain, I wondered if Travis was about to appear.   I felt bad about everything that had happened to Travis when he was alive, but he still terrified me, even the times he helped me. It's true that I faced my fears, but I was frightened the whole time.

I never wanted to break my neck or die or come back from the dead with a ghost. I never asked for any of this and I don't understand why it happened to me. I know Mrs. Grey had called it a gift, but there's no way that I could say it was.

If there was anything that I regretted, it was not thinking sooner about my dad. I could have asked Travis earlier and maybe have gotten a better answer than 'hope' from him. I wondered about him even more now that I was no longer being haunted.

Most of the time now, I just try to be normal and not to think about all of it too much. But sometimes at night, in bed, with the lights out, before I drift off to sleep, I'll look over at my copy of *Tom Sawyer* on the nightstand, and I can't help thinking back on all of the strange events that have happened.

Chapter 70

Columbus Day weekend had finally arrived and with it came a three-day weekend. Tom and his family invited me and Rosie to go with them to a camp they had on Lake Ontario. Twice a year we would go with them to the camp and Columbus Day weekend was always the last time for the year.

It sounds funny but one of my favorite parts of the trip was the last mile of the drive. The city would give way to long stretches of country roads and small towns. At the very end we turned down an old road shadowed by pine trees on either side. We would go up a small hill and at the top, the sky and the lake merged together blue. With the windows open and the fresh smell of the water and pines drifting through the car, I always knew camp was around the next turn.

The camp sat alone at the end of the road on the water's edge. It looked a lot like an old house. It had three small bedrooms, a living room and kitchen and a big porch that overlooked the lake. There was a small sandy beach and a short dock off to the side with a row boat attached to it. Each year we would fish and swim and roast marshmallows. It was always fun.

After unpacking and getting a fire started for hot dogs, Rosie, Tom and I went down to the lake to swim. The water was really cold in October, but that didn't stop us from jumping right in. Tom had diving rings and he scattered them about and we all split up to find them underwater.

I swam out to where one of the rings had

splashed in and dove down. I felt my ears fill with water and felt the pressure of the frigid lake upon me. Still, I continued to make my way toward the dark, sandy bottom. I suddenly realized that this was the first time since my accident that I had been swimming and underwater. Just as the diving ring became visible, panic began to sweep through my body. I had to get to the surface. I tried to push up from the bottom but my feet missed. I struggled, my arms and legs flailing in the dense, dark water.

Finally, I broke through and gasped loudly for air. Waves of the cold lake water lapped against my face as I struggled to move closer to shore, and be able to stand on the sandy bottom. My hands were shaking as a cold breeze drifted in over the lake. I felt my lips begin to quiver, either from the cold or the panic...or both.

I saw the camp porch straight ahead and was beginning to catch my breath when something caught my eye in a row of pine trees off to the right. Standing in the shadow of a pine tree, was a little girl with long black hair wearing a red dress. I could see her clear as day. I knew that Tom's camp sat all alone and I wondered how she had gotten here and if she was lost.

"Hey?" I half asked, not really knowing what to say.

The girl did not respond or move.

"Mikey?" I heard off in the distance.

"Mikey?" came the voice again.

I turned to see Tom and Rosie staring at me.

"What are you doing, Zombie?" asked Tom.

"Who's the little girl?" I asked turning back to the woods. She was gone. My arms began to shiver.

Tom and Rosie looked beyond me seeing nothing in the woods. "Other than you, there aren't any little girls around here," Tom said. "We're the only camp around for miles."

Tom and Rosie laughed, then dove back under water to retrieve the rest of the rings. I looked back to the empty woods. Just as I was thinking that it must have been my imagination. I heard the wind carry the sing-song laughter of a little girl.

"No, no, no!" was all I could say.

A sinking feeling filled my chest as I realized

that the air itself had become colder than the water.

That could only mean one thing.

There was another ghost.

THE END

ABOUT THE AUTHOR

They Call Me Zombie is John Mercer's first novel. John is a sixth grade English teacher. He lives in Fulton, New York with his family.

To learn more about They Call Me Zombie and John, visit the They Call Me Zombie Facebook page.